IN THE NAME OF THE GUN

Nobody saw him appear, but suddenly he was there on the street, the rising sun at his back casting his shadow across the dust. 'Shiloh!' Either one man called his name or a dozen whispered it at once. That single word saw Cleveland Kain step from the alley, .45 glinting in the early light. 'Shiloh can't beat Kain,' gasped the judge. 'Nobody can.' 'Can and will!' Shakespeare Jones said loudly. Then whispered: 'If he doesn't this town is doomed!'

RYAN BODIE

IN THE NAME OF THE GUN

Complete and Unabridged

LINFORD
Leicester

First published in Great Britain in 2008 by
Robert Hale Limited
London

First Linford Edition
published 2009
by arrangement with
Robert Hale Limited
London

British Library CIP Data

Bodie, Ryan.
   In the name of the gun - -
   (Linford western library)
   1. Western stories.
   2. Large type books.
   I. Title II. Series
   823.9'2–dc22

   ISBN 978–1–84782–735–7

Published by
F. A. Thorpe (Publishing)
Anstey, Leicestershire

Set by Words & Graphics Ltd.
Anstey, Leicestershire
Printed and bound in Great Britain by
T. J. International Ltd., Padstow, Cornwall

1

The Killing Ground

Dirty weather was building up as Clint Shiloh pushed Two Bits in the direction of the valley. A gusty wind tainted with cold came down off the high country. Piled-up cloud masses swirled over the rocky shoulders of distant mountain tops and the wind chattered like a telegraph key in the wintry branches overhead.

There were damp patches on the horseman's shoulders and beard stubble darkened lean cheeks. He had gone without sleep to stay on the killer's trail and the gruelling pace was at last beginning to tell. Yet reminding himself of the $500 the job would pay succeeded in giving his spirits a lift again.

In the mountain town of Toprock, Shiloh missed the man he hunted by half a day. Clage Cantrell had pulled out at daybreak, they told him, heading in the direction of Tincup down in the valley. So the gunfighter had swung up again and rode out under the watchful eyes of a town relieved to see the last of him. He hadn't said who he was, and there was no need. He was a young man with the wolf look, who wore his six-shooter strapped low on his thigh.

'Gunfighter!' sniffed the plain folk of Toprock, and they were right about that. The Clint Shilohs of the West were a breed apart.

He lighted a cigarette and gusted smoke into the cold air.

He knew Cantrell was aware he was being tailed, for the killer wasn't stopping at any one place one minute longer than he must. Shiloh figured he was hoping to make it through all the way to Utah. Joel Dunstan told him the killer had friends in the Dakotas. Dunstan was the cattleman who'd put up the $500 reward after Cantrell had gunned down his son at Boulder City's Crazy Horse Saloon in a quarrel over a half-witted percentage girl. An 18-year-old kid stacked up against a veteran hardcase with seven notches on his gun handles was no gunfight. It was murder.

But the hawk had slain the blue jay and now they were sending the hunting falcon after the hawk.

Out of the higher country by now and quartering south-east, Shiloh raised sign that told him he was nearing civilization again. Stock had been herded into that box canyon up ahead some time recent. Wagons had passed where the trails forked yonder. He sighted the burned out remnants of a campfire where cowboys had cooked a meal.

He stopped by the stream to water the horse, then pushed on as early dusk began to drift down over the chilled landscape. The way led sharply down to the valley floor, twisting in and out, following the contours of the hills.

Trees dotted the slopes, giant blue cedars bending in the stiff winds. But Clint Shiloh wasn't interested in scenery. He was studying the rider coming towards him along the lonesome trail. He watched the man carefully, for in his business it never paid to take chances.

Now the rider was closer the gunfighter saw he was a mountain man, a hulking, shaggy relic of a fast-vanishing race astride a hard-eyed monster of a Cheyenne gelding, untrimmed since last winter. The wind tossed the horse's flowing mane and fluttered the rider's spotted kerchief as he made to ride on by. But the gunfighter halted him with a lazy lift of the hand. There was silky authority in Clint Shiloh's every movement.

'That Tincup?' He didn't look at the man as he spoke. His gaze was fixed upon the distant coils of wood smoke rising above the trees up ahead.

'Yeah, that's her.'

'I'm looking for a man.'

'Don't surprise me none.'

A mocking amusement touched the gunfighter's face as he looked at the man. 'Now don't get mouthy, squaw man. No call for that.'

The mountain man flushed and the big, vein-corded hands upon the saddle pommel gripped hard.

Shiloh knew the breed. They were tough, hard and brave. Their idea of a man was one who could fight — kick, gouge, head-butt — until the sun went down. Their pride was in their sinews; they saw no honour in a gun. They were part of a simpler world that was being overrun by a breed of men they didn't understand or like. They had been kings of the West once, but now the new rulers were swifter, younger men with tied-down guns.

'Clage Cantrell is this man's name,' Shiloh said softly. 'Tall, red hair, horse teeth?'

'Mebbe I seen him, mebbe I didn't.'

That was good enough. He knew he'd seen his killer sure enough. Clint Shiloh smiled, showing strong white teeth beneath his trimmed moustache.

'Much obliged, friend. You can mosey along now.'

The big Cheyenne gelding moved

past with an old-fashioned Sharps rifle jutting from a worn yellow saddle scabbard. A short distance on, the mountain man hipped around and yelled, 'You just might find a whole heap more than you're bargaining for down there, gunman.'

'Good hunting, friend!' Shiloh called back and rode on.

The gunfighter's smile slowly faded. The mountain man had reminded him of his father. Bartholomew Shiloh, half-breed hunter, had worked for the big fur brigades from Montana down to the Mississippi Basin. The old man died when Shiloh was just a kid and he recalled him only in fragmented flashes of memory.

Most clearly he recalled his strength, his love of combat and his fierce pride. 'One at a time!' he would bawl when his sharp tongue or overbearing ways touched off a ruckus. 'One at a time or all together, it makes no difference to Bartholomew Shiloh!' And would then proceed to bang heads together and kick out savagely with his big caulked boots.

That vanishing breed, once essential to the fur trade, had been unable to adapt when the old wild days were gone. He'd had too much power and strength, far too much cruelty. On a regular basis he broke the new laws and fought with men wearing badges. The mountain man's life was simple and direct and they recognized no peer. In the cruel mountains there was danger and violent death at every turn. The only rewards he'd sought were a full belly, whiskey when he needed it, and a woman handy to bring him comfort.

One day, a serious man with a star on his vest came to visit Shiloh's father. There had been the matter of a shooting. The old man would have to face trial. No, no goddamn trial! Heated words, then the ugly term, 'Half-breed!' The old man had jerked out a pistol and shot the sheriff down. Then he went off to the saloon to visit with his latest girlfriend, a fat woman with bright flowers in her hair.

Clint Shiloh never saw his father again. The possemen had come to take him away and hang him, leaving behind a half-grown kid alone in the world with just the two legacies, a Colt .45 and the skill to use it . . .

Not much, but it proved to be enough.

Darkness fell as the solitary rider crossed the creaking bridge that led into Tincup's crooked main stem. He heard music drifting on the wind and sighted a long, unpainted hall with bright lights shimmering. The music was coming from the hall and people were going in from the street. Tincup was holding a dance.

He slowed his horse. He could be a man of sudden impulses — just like his old man, he often mused. He might follow a man's trail relentlessly for long days, letting neither the miles nor fatigue slow him down. Then bright music and the sight of pretty girls in long dresses twirling around a dance floor would arouse pleasure and excitement, erasing all else from his mind.

Sometimes, that was. Not often.

Setting his jaw, he rode on to check out in turn saloon, hotel, livery stable. No sign of Cantrell.

He reckoned his man had likely moved right on, yet could just as easily be holed up someplace near. He sensed that his sudden arrival made the townsfolk edgy. It might be smart to relax a little and give them time to get used to him, then go sniffing around after that. Who could tell? Maybe Cantrell would come looking for him if he stayed put. He'd had it happen that way before. They got so damned nervous they couldn't stand it. So they had to come after you, hoping to catch you off guard.

He rode back to the dance hall and stepped down.

A pair of gaunt young toughs lounging on the porch studied him closely as he stood below them, tapping his foot in time to 'Johnny in the Low

Ground' coming from within. The two were plainly small-time, though he'd glimpsed a few in the saloon who'd surprised him — hardcases with a confidence you didn't expect to find in a place like Tincup. He detected a faint whiff of danger in this wind-blown night now as he jumped lithely up on to the gallery and went in.

He stepped into the light, arms swinging loosely. His formidable appearance attracted the attention of a fat man in a well-tailored suit, who said, 'Two bits admission, stranger.'

Shiloh toyed with the notion of telling him to go straight to hell, just to see his reaction. Then he spotted the girl in the green dress and tugged a quarter from his pocket and flipped it to the fat man without looking.

Her golden hair was fastened to the nape of her neck with pink ribbon. She had been dancing with a yokel in striped trousers. But during the brief intermission as a man went round the floor shaking wax from a container on to the boards, she stood with two skinny girls near the punchbowl.

She glanced his way and he smiled, causing her to blush in confusion and turn away. The orchestra, comprising guitar, piano, fiddle and bass, launched into a waltz and he started across the floor.

A young man in a bright yellow shirt reached her first. The fellow scowled when the gunfighter's hand grasped his shoulder. The scowl failed to hold when he found himself staring into Clint Shiloh's dark eyes.

'Sorry, friend,' Shiloh said with an amiable grin. 'The next one's yours, maybe.'

Yellow Shirt hesitated. Then an elbow jabbed him just beneath the armpit and he bit off a curse as the gunfighter, moving silkily past him, took the girl in his arms and they glided off beneath the lights.

She was truly pretty, he realized. Country all the way with healthy round arms and fine cheekbones.

He was a good dancer and she had no trouble following him. Curious eyes followed them as they glided past under the lights.

Suddenly she said, 'You're the gunfighter, aren't you?'

'Gunfighter? What gunfighter?'

'They were talking about you before you came in.'

'Not saying anything good, I hope?'

'Is there anything good to be said about a gunfighter?'

He held her a little closer, in no way put off by her attitude. He could tell she was interested. He liked her poise, the cool way she treated him.

'You sound to me like a girl who might know something about fast guns,' he said.

'I wouldn't know the fast from the slow,' she replied. And then, quite suddenly her pose collapsed. 'You're in great danger here!' she hissed urgently. 'Don't you realize that?'

Clint Shiloh's faint smile stirred the edges of his silky moustache. 'Why — I

12

always am, blue-eyes, I just naturally always am.'

She didn't say more yet he felt the tension in her body. Shiloh danced on smoothly, outwardly relaxed but with every sense razor alert as they continued to glide around the floor. This was the kind of situation he enjoyed — snatching pleasure while the stink of danger poisoned the very air. In turn, he studied her pale face, their fellow dancers, the stag line by the door and the long row of red-cheeked country women sitting along the side benches.

In that moment he was acutely aware of everything — the lights, the colours, the smell of perfume, the glimmer of glassware. But all the time, the music appeared to be keeping time with that slow, warning ticking inside his skull.

The waltz finished abruptly and the dancers began changing partners. The girl made to move away but he held her. She stared at him uncertainly, then half-smiled.

Next moment a hand dropped on his shoulder.

'Mine, mister.'

It was the man in the yellow shirt.

'You're mistaken,' Clint Shiloh said. 'Blue-eyes and me are going around again.'

'This is a change-partners, Bucko,' the man said, red-faced, and the hand on his shoulder began to push. 'So this dance is m — '

Shiloh's right fist blurred. The man staggered back so fast he tripped over a stool and thudded to the floor on the broad of his back.

The music stopped.

'What's the meaning of this?' a bustling official demanded, striding up. 'I don't care who you are, stranger, you can't carry on like that in here.'

Shiloh still stood with one arm about the young woman's waist.

'Tell the band to play 'Cornpone Yellow',' he said. He didn't raise his voice but his flat stare held the fat man motionless until he began to fidget. The man he'd punched was struggling to his feet with a thin trickle of crimson running from the corner of his mouth. The fat man glanced uneasily at Shiloh, then sighed and nodded to the band.

The strains of 'Cornpone Yellow' filled the room. Shiloh bowed and was about to take the girl in his arms once more when he glimpsed the face in back of the crowd that filled the entrance. It was a bony face beneath a shock of red hair. And he caught a glimpse of horse teeth.

'Sorry, pretty girl,' he breathed, 'but seems like you'll have to excuse me after all.'

Impulsively, as though scenting danger, she reached out and clutched at his sleeve. 'No, please stay here and have this dance with me.'

He wanted to. For it seemed he did not repel her even though she must surely know what he was. He reckoned she genuinely wanted him to stay.

'You can do better than me, blue

eyes,' he said softly. 'You can do a whole lot better.'

Then he was stepping away from her, an easy-moving man with his gaze now focused upon the crowd in the doorway.

Cantrell was no longer to be seen.

The crowd parted quickly at his approach. As he gained the landing outside he sighted a tall, high-shouldered figure swiftly receding along the crooked street some fifty yards distant.

'Cantrell!'

The killer shot a glance back over his shoulder but kept walking. Faster now. Shiloh sprang lightly down from the landing, cut out into the centre of the street and followed. Just as fast. A stiff wind fluttered the bandanna at his throat and snatched up a grimy sheet of newspaper ahead of him and wrapped it around a telegraph pole. He strode on by the blacksmith's, the freight depot and the tall building that bore the faded legend, Western Palace.

He was not making up any ground.

Cantrell, tall and lean with trouser legs flapping against skinny shanks, was swift and light-footed. As he passed beneath a street light his badly trimmed red beard seemed to glow. The man's riding boots thudded upon the plank-walk but Shiloh's own steps made no sound in the deep dust of the road. His right hand swung close to the hip, ready to reach for iron in an instant. Where was Cantrell heading? He sensed he wasn't simply running blind . . .

The man's steps finally began to slow some two blocks away from the dance hall. Then he halted abruptly before the unpainted, two-storey edifice of the Tincup Hotel.

When Cantrell swung about to face him squarely with his back pressed against the hotel wall, Shiloh slowed some but kept coming.

'I'm tuckered out from running, Shiloh!' Cantrell's voice was uneven.

Shiloh's gaze flicked suspiciously over false-fronts and alleys, probing deep wells of black shadow.

'And I'm tired of chasing you, Cantrell!'

He halted, shoulders relaxed, hands hanging loosely at his sides. The wind made a small humming sound as it feathered his stiff hatbrim. An ancient blue dog lurking beneath the raised porch rose stiffly and moved slowly away, rolling its eyes. Clage Cantrell stood firm, surprisingly so.

'So, this is it, Shiloh?'

He nodded. 'If you're thinking of making a play, Cantrell, just remember you made your name shooting boys. I wear full-size boots.'

The outlaw made no move towards the gun hanging at his side. He seemed to be waiting for something. When he shot a jittery look over one shoulder, Shiloh felt his impatience mount.

'Let's get it over with, killer. Either toss that cutter or use it!'

Something sick crossed Cantrell's horse features, a look Shiloh could not accurately read. Then without warning, the man grabbed six-gun handle.

Instantly, Shiloh drew with the blinding speed that had bested far better men than the one facing him now.

He triggered just once.

Cantrell's gun went off. A moment later, Shiloh's bullet slammed him back into the hotel wall. The outlaw remained pinned there for a long moment with the smoking gun dangling from his hand. Then he buckled and fell, staring down at the last thing he would ever see — Shiloh's bullet-hole in the breast pocket of his greasy shirt.

The echoes of the shot welled up then faded away. Shiloh holstered. He stared at the dead man and felt nothing. Then a sound from the hotel brought his head up sharply.

He froze as the four men who had risen from cover behind the solid timber balustrade of the hotel's upper veranda came fully erect behind the Colt .45s gripped in steady hands. One was the man in the yellow shirt from the dance hall.

He sucked in a breath as a fifth figure

appeared further along. This man was tall and dapper with an impressive bearing. He moved confidently to stand in the full glare of the light washing up from the street. With a derby hat cocked over one eye, he folded his arms and gave the faintest of smiles when he spoke.

'Shiloh!'

Just the single word.

Shiloh showed no reaction, still had not moved. There was no regret in him. No fear. He'd walked into something that appeared dangerous, but he was unfazed, even fatalistic. If gunpowder should burn he'd execute his best-ever draw and nail one for sure, maybe more. But that would be about the limit. His first target would be this tall big-noter in the tailored suit. He'd never had time for the wealthy well-bred breed, and that went double when they came backed up by guns.

The tall man cut a glance to Cantrell's crumpled body lying directly beneath him in a pool of blood. He nodded. 'Cantrell said you were very good, Shiloh.' A thin smile. 'But as I rarely take any man's word on anything, I held my boys back to test you to the limit, if need be. I'm pleased to say you proved worthy of your reputation.'

A flicker of annoyance stirred the man's chiselled features when Shiloh remained silent and impassive.

'Very fast — but perhaps too damned arrogant if I'm any judge!' the tall man snapped. 'But I take it you accept the fact I hold your life in my hands right now? That one word from me will guarantee your funeral will make two tomorrow and not just the one?'

'It could end up more than two — counting yourself, dude,' Clint answered. Then he nodded. 'But, yeah, I'll allow you've played your hand well and have the drop. So. What comes next?'

The man smiled, gave a laconic signal with his left hand and immediately the covering guns were lifted.

'What now? Why, we talk, Clint Shiloh. What else?'

2

Contract to Kill

His name was Marcus Whitman and his office at the Tincup Hotel was large and cluttered by furniture, filing cabinets, stuffed pigeon-holes and a big and battered old desk where a brass-shaded lamp burned brightly.

It looked like the quarters of some high-powered businessman, Shiloh mused. But Whitman was far more than that. The gunfighter had heard he played politics like a gambler and was rumoured to have had people who crossed him eliminated as he'd sought political power and success back in Denver.

Smoke from their cigarettes hung heavy in the air, drifting about the lamp. Elbows upon the desk, Whitman was informing Shiloh in the direct brisk way he had that, although he'd been a successful land and property dealer, these days he was a fulltime politician 'climbing the ladder to the State legislature', as he phrased it — very plainly enjoying the role of a successful man on the rise with a finger in many an important pie.

Shiloh sat in profile from the man across the desk, one leg crossed over the other, a cigarette angled from his teeth and eyes deceptively sleepy. The overhead light gleamed softly on his thick dark hair and smooth moustache.

In back of the gunfighter, Whitman's gun-handlers stood lounging against the wall guarding the room's single door.

Emil Durkin was a large man with powerful, hairy hands and a brutal underlip. Cut Woodstock, as tall as Whitman, was muscular and lithe-moving with eyes the colour of faded chips of slate. Jack Curran was an impassive block, while the fourth member of the pack, Harris, was simply ugly and appeared unwashed.

Whitman seemed pleased with the purring sound of his own voice as he informed his visitor of the hardships and disappointments of a politico's life in these troubled times.

Earlier, Shiloh had stood by while the man had authoritatively dealt with the local sheriff in regard to the shooting. The lawman was deferential and seemed quite pleased to have been handed responsibility for the deceased outlaw, widely wanted with a large reward to be claimed.

Soon Whitman was beginning to bore him with his boasting and grand plans. Yet Shiloh was patient. He scented maybe both money and opportunity in the air if he were patient. He didn't believe Whitman had stage-managed that show of strength on the street just for the fun of it. This man wanted something. Shiloh was curious but didn't let it show. Yet some of his boredom finally showed through, and the other noticed.

'All right, down to business,' he said

briskly. 'You're likely wondering where all this talk is leading us, Shiloh.'

'Let me guess.'

'Go ahead.'

'You want to hire my gun.' Shiloh gave a small smile. 'Don't be surprised. That's the only reason men like you ever sit down to talk with men like me, Whitman. So, why don't we cut the jawbone and get down to cases?'

'If you insist. But I prefer to be referred to as Mr Whitman.'

'Fine. You can call me Mr Shiloh.'

A gunman stirred. Whitman studied Shiloh for a long moment's silence. He was arrogant and fiery by nature, yet was disciplined enough to accept insolence or offence when playing for big stakes. He managed a tight smile as he leaned back in his chair.

'Uh-huh, the more I see of you. Shiloh, the more I realize you are certainly the man.' Then briskly 'Very well, let's talk business. First, the Cantrell affair. Doubtless you're curious about that?'

Shiloh just shrugged.

'Of course you are. Well, Cantrell rode in to see me this afternoon after hearing I was hiring guns. He fitted the brand, so I gave him a good hearing. While we talked he revealed you were hard on his tracks, also that he was wanted for murder. I was immediately interested. Why? Well, I'd already heard about you and your skills, so I hatched a little plan whereby I might get to see if you were as big as your reputation — with the help of one dumb outlaw.'

Whitman paused to ash his cigar, then went on. 'I suggested to Cantrell that, for a fee, my boys here would take care of you for him if he simply drew you out on to the street for them. Rather enterprising of me, don't you think?'

'Maybe.'

Whitman spread his hands. 'Of course it was. What better way to assess the talents of two men than have them shoot it out?'

'Keep talking.'

The man spread his hands. 'I set up my boys on the street. Cantrell believed they would gun you down when he led you to the spot.' A pause to smile. 'He must have died both surprised and bitterly disappointed by my deception, don't you think?'

'I'm not paid to think. But a man doesn't have to be a thinker to see through you, Whitman. You tested me out, on the street. So now you know I'm fast — who do you want killed?'

'I knew you were a smart one! All right — it's Ford Gabriel.' Whitman wasn't smiling any longer.

Shiloh straightened in the battered horsehair chair. 'You did say Gabriel?'

'You've heard of him, obviously?'

He nodded. There wasn't anyone in the fast-gun trade unfamiliar with that name. Gabriel had been one of the top guns in the business before dropping out of circulation. Shiloh had never met the man but a wanted photograph had shown a husky-looking hardcase with unusual eyes — proud, cold, and supremely confident. The eyes of a genuine gunslinger or he was no judge.

'I've heard of him,' Shiloh drawled. 'Where does he hang his hat these days?'

'In my territory.'

'Your territory?'

'Well, it's mine in a political sense. Or will be.'

Whitman rose suddenly to jerk down a wall map. He jabbed at it with his cigar.

'Clearwater County in the lower Celinda Mountains, some fifty miles north-east of here. Sparsely settled but for the War God Hills section up in the high country. The War Gods boast some of the finest country in the region and have been opened up for close settlement and is now officially on the voting register as a result. It boasts a sizeable town, Durant. The rest of that region is just a scatter with a few hamlets apart from Durant, and there's a hardcase place name of Sweet Creek down along the wagon trail. I've won the right to stand for election to the territorial legislature providing I can carry Clearwater County in the upcoming elections.'

'But?' the gunfighter prompted when he fell silent. 'There was a 'but' in your voice just then.'

'But it's not all plain sailing.'

'How come?'

Whitman returned to his desk and dropped into his chair.

'Every damn thing went wrong when I visited the county last to announce my candidacy for the legislature. There was trouble with touchy Durant towners and some ranchers. Resentment, misunderstandings, suspicion and antagonism. I encountered them all. Ungrateful hicks! There was I attempting to do something for them and put their county on the map, and they resented it, even hated me!'

The man acted as though unable to understand this reaction. Shiloh comprehended it all right, Whitman was plainly an arrogant go-getter. But that was nothing to him. A job was a job, and Whitman looked big dollars.

'And?' he grunted.

Whitman studied the gunfighter with bleak eyes.

'And then came Gabriel, mister. Don't ask me why or how, but suddenly some months back when I was visiting, this Gabriel showed up in Durant. One of my men, Pardee, got involved in an argument with a citizen. Blows were struck. Gabriel called Pardee out and shot him down, then ordered me out. Me! He had the gall to order me out of the county I plan to represent in the elections!'

'So you left, I take it?'

'I left — after having three valuable men shot up. Several times since, I've attempted to return, and each time I've been blocked or driven off. Gabriel has established himself as their friend and protector up in the War God Hills where all my potential voters are — low-life gunslinging son of a bitch!'

The gunfighter had no trouble in figuring where all this was leading.

'So, you want me to take care of Gabriel?' he said abruptly.

Whitman appeared both surprised and deeply impressed.

'Why . . . yes. That is precisely what I — '

'All right.'

Whitman blinked. 'Just like that? No worry about going up against a top guntipper like that? No haggling over money?'

The gunfighter's steady gaze fixed upon Whitman's smooth face.

'I don't haggle.'

'Well, I'll be damned!'

'Doubtless, doubtless . . . ' Shiloh rose smoothly and scooped up his hat. 'Two hundred down and another three when I've finished the job.'

Plainly delighted, Whitman sprang to his feet. 'I'll meet you a week from today at Sweet Creek at the foot of the high country — after the job is done. See, that's the sort of confidence I have in you already. So, it's a deal?'

'Sure.'

'Done then. But there's just one more thing. I don't want anyone to know you're working for me. I have my reasons for that.'

'Don't fret. I'll be working, not talking.'

Whitman counted out the $200 and Shiloh turned to go. With the deal finalized, he wanted to be gone from this smoky room. He rarely respected clients and Whitman was no exception. They tagged many an ugly name on to gunfighters, but at least they had the guts to risk their lives to earn the gold. The Whitmans of the world hid behind their money and let other men be brave for them. Their breed was essential to Shiloh's way of life but he didn't have to like them.

Emil Durkin lounged against the closed door. He didn't move as Shiloh approached. He motioned him aside but the heavyweight stayed put.

'Mr Whitman ain't said as how you're free to go as yet, gun punk.'

Shiloh struck without warning. A

pistoning right hook crashed into a stubbled jaw with an ugly sound. Durkin's big head was smashed back against the hard cedar door and he fell forward with a crash and didn't move. Shiloh swung to face Whitman, who'd leapt from his chair, outraged.

'Relax, Whitman.'

'You — you savage!' Whitman accused. 'There was no call for that.'

'I'm particular how folks talk to me. If that bothers you, better say so now.'

For a long moment they stood facing, the dapper man with the money and power, the young man with the dark eyes and the gun.

Whitman dragged the back of his hand across his mouth, sensing the full menace of this man for the first time. 'Very well, gunman. I can only hope you display such efficiency against Gabriel when you come face to face.'

'You let me handle that job of work. Just be at Sweet Creek with the $300 in a week's time. That's all you have to fret about.'

He raked the others with a bleak stare, then turned, kicked the unconscious man's legs aside and went out.

They had removed Cantrell's body from the street when he appeared. Standing in the doorway, Shiloh paused to glance along the street where a knot of men stood talking before a building which had the words 'Lucius Grey Undertaker' painted in gold letters upon the window.

His eyes lingered momentarily upon the dark stain on the earth by the hitch-rack before he shrugged, swung away and started off for the livery stables.

The big-nosed liveryman was eager to talk but Shiloh was not.

Astride Two Bits, he rode into the next street and followed it, heading out the way he'd arrived. People were walking home from the dance. They appeared subdued as a consequence of the violence earlier. A couple was passing the barber shop, hand in hand. He saw a yellow shirt and a green dress.

Shiloh checked his mount.

The girl sighted him and immediately halted. The man in the yellow shirt looked nervous, but the gunfighter's gaze was fixed upon the girl. The loathing and contempt he read in her delicate face now wounded him the way a bullet never could. That look struck deep into his loneliness, and for a moment he was no longer Clint Shiloh, gunfighter, but just a young man full of vague yearnings for something he could never hope to have.

With a look, he attempted to make her understand how it was with a man like himself. How his gun was necessary in these lands beyond the law. But she was simply a clean, country-bred girl who knew only right from wrong. She saw him as wrong and beyond redemption or understanding.

How could someone like that even begin to understand what it was like to be reared in a totally savage world? he brooded.

The couple passed on quickly,

leaving him motionless in the saddle, the breath running in and out of him in long, slow gusts. He finally stirred, his features haggard now as he jerked on the reins to turn back to the saloon. He dismounted and went inside to buy a bottle of sourmash whiskey from a barkeep who placed his change down on the bartop as if afraid to touch his hand.

Then he rode out hard.

⋆ ⋆ ⋆

He'd finished the bottle of sourmash before reaching Fort Brodie. He had a foggy impression of teetering false-fronts, rumbling freighter wheels, dim lights which seemed to tremble from the pounding of a hammer as a smithy toiled into the night.

He stabled Two Bits and made his unsteady way for the saloon to buy another bottle before checking into the hotel, where he spent the night.

Breakfast was taken at a sleazy eatery

on the main stem, then he was drumming north-east again.

He travelled the long horse miles slowly now, burdened with a strange depression. The country here was flat, sweeping off into bays of buffalo grass and dotted by pine and scrub cedar with the occasional patch of mescal.

Once a buzzard glided overhead too low and his gun jerked from leather to roar just once, plucking the bird from the sky. 'Loser!' he jeered as the last black feathers fluttered down. Two Bits rolled his eyes back at him as if in reproof.

As the day wore on his depression began to lift.

He was crossing hill country now where the air was pure and sweet. He inhaled the fragrance and felt his spirits rise. Flexing arms and shoulders he relished the sensation of strength and suppleness in his body. He squared his shoulders and unbuttoned his black shirt to the breeze. The wind was in his hair and he was Clint Shiloh, the loner who made his own rules and called no man master.

He finally stopped to rest within sight of the mountains with timber clothing their slopes. To the south lay rimrock.

With his head clear again he seemed to be seeing it all for the first time. Grassy foothills rolled away to his right, the colouring deeper by the creek banks. A flock of geese drifted high overhead with a mournful honking, and a long way off, buffalo moved slowly like a gentle brown flood against the green.

He ate a meal of canned meat and topped it off with a Red Man cigar and black coffee. He rubbed the horse down, fed it a hatful of corn, and cleaned his .45. He rode on through the changing country and before nightfall had reached the squalid little flatland town on the wagon trail that was Sweet Creek, lying on the border of Clearwater County, his destination. Just a handful of solid houses surrounded by a scatter of unpainted frame buildings crouched at the base of the Celinda Mountains and the War God Hills.

'Yes, sir,' the liveryman assured him around a mouthful of plug tobacco, 'that pass yonder takes you right up into the War Gods and Durant, mister. Er, you got business up in them parts, stranger?'

'Yeah . . . business . . .'

★ ★ ★

The wind was uncertain as it often could be just before dawn. It rustled in the dark pines clothing the upper reaches of Cottonwood Pass and blew away the thin mists.

The high country landscape appeared peaceful but the rider knew this to be false. There was little law in the county and none up here. Clearwater County lay eighty miles from the nearest sheriff's office and over one hundred from a court of law.

The settlers here were hardy and enterprising and largely lived by their own laws. A man looked out for himself and his own with guts and a gun. If he couldn't manage that, he had come too far west.

The morning light began as a thin grey bar along the rimrock, then spread slowly upwards into the east, while the western sky remained dark. The sound of birds heralded the rising sun, and as first light spread down over the War God Hills the wind faded off and the sound of his hoofbeats drifted up the high country trail.

The lone rider appeared along the yellow ribbon of road, paused momentarily to take his bearings, then moved on to reach the fringe of his destination, the level highlands and fine cattle lands.

The land quickly levelled out into rolling rangeland cupped by rearing mountains. Cattle dotted the green open spaces and a thin plume of smoke rose from a ranch house out of sight beyond a fold in the land.

He drifted past set-back ranch buildings and squat yellow haystacks, and the climb was a full mile behind him before Shiloh spotted the rider.

The man was travelling along a low humpback ridge to his right some two hundred yards distant and moving at his same pace, travelling parallel.

A sure instinct told him this was the man he'd come to confront. He'd never expected to arrive here before they'd heard about him first. Things didn't work that way. People talked and secrets leaked out, and a man learned to take that in his stride.

For all its attractiveness, this was a land beyond law. Once a year — maybe — a posse of lawmen or an official serving a writ, might make it this far into the far regions. For the rest of the time, a man's integrity and grit, his friends and the gun he carried were his only protection.

Unless, of course, folks might get together and hire someone to look out for them. A man with a gun being the only law up here.

He could just see from that shadowy

silhouette through the trees that the slow-moving horseman was strongly built and sat his saddle with the self-assurance that came naturally to men of the gun, like Ford Gabriel.

And Clint Shiloh.

Whether Gabriel was hero, villain or something in between was of no interest to the gunfighter. Men with money and power wanted him gone. That was all he needed to know, although he did recall hearing that many up here actually lived in fear of Gabriel. But it seemed he was in favour with the men who wielded the power in Durant.

He smiled cynically. Men with power made their own laws just about everywhere, he mused. He took out a cigar, set it alight and continued on steadily with smoke drifting back over his shoulder.

* * *

A half-mile further on and his 'shadow' was still with him. He now caught the occasional glitter of sunlight on harness and cartridge rims. Some distance ahead the humpback finally levelled out some and the trail he followed curved around towards it to form a junction. Should each continue the way he was heading they would converge near that stand of aspen yonder.

It was Gabriel, of course.

Shiloh confirmed it the moment the rider emerged fully from the scattered timber that had separated them, still moving at his slow deliberate pace. Fast Ford, they called him. Maybe he was fast. But how fast was fast enough? Often a man didn't discover the answer to that curly one until showdown time, by which time it could prove too late to quit, and often did.

Now the riders began to converge more quickly. Shiloh drew on his cigar, savouring the flavour of rich tobacco. He could hear the creak of the other's saddle leather by this. He saw that Gabriel was impressively well built. He sported plain moleskin pants, faded blue shirt and low-crowned Stetson.

Nothing flashy about Fast Ford.

Reaching the aspen stand first, Shiloh reined in and turned. The horseman approached across the dew-damp grass and Shiloh felt the full impact of his stare. He flicked his cheroot away and rested both hands on saddle pommel as the man drew rein.

'Who are you?' Gabriel was plainly not a man to mince words.

'Shiloh.'

'Clint Shiloh?'

'You've got me fitted right. And you're Ford Gabriel?'

The man nodded, his eyes raking Shiloh head to toe.

'You look like you come expensive, Shiloh. How much is he paying you?'

Shiloh's jaw was setting hard. 'Could be you talk too much, mister.'

Of a sudden, his voice and manner were icy. He didn't believe in dragging these things out, or trying to score some advantage before the guns. He was ready, had been since the moment they sighted one another.

Gabriel nodded to himself as though in acknowledgement of some eternal truth.

'You figure you can beat me, Shiloh?'

'No.'

This caused surprise. 'No?'

'I don't reckon I can — I know it!'

Responding instantly, Ford Gabriel swung to ground and stepped away from his horse. Unhurriedly, Shiloh followed suit. They stood facing and the new morning was gently beautiful all around them.

'I ain't the talkative kind, Shiloh. So I'll just say this. Whatever Whitman is paying you it ain't enough. Ride out or they'll bury you where you stand.'

This was an old scene for Clint Shiloh, seemingly older than God. His last gunfight was on a squalid street, this was all gentle sunshine on a yellow-dust trail flanked by pine and aspen — as he spread his feet and flexed supple fingers.

'Ready when you are,' was his soft response.

Gabriel nodded solemnly as though in acknowledgement of an eternal truth.

No more words.

They stood facing for a timeless moment, then erupted into blistering action. Hands blurred downwards and swept up clutching long-barrelled revolvers which instantly filled the world with their savage voices.

Shiloh felt lead tug at his hatbrim. His own bullet struck Gabriel squarely in the chest, smashing him backwards as though struck by a giant's fist. The man attempted to trigger one last time but that was already beyond him. He was past everything but the ability to remain standing for unsteady moments before curving slowly forwards, dead before he struck ground.

Shiloh stared at the motionless figure and slowly tugged off his hat. That slug had carved a neat half-circle from the brim. He fingered the side of his head and loose hair came away. Whoever had dabbed him Fast Ford wasn't wrong.

He replaced his hat before lifting the dead man to drape him across his saddle, conscious of the massive silence that came in the wake of roaring guns.

He shook himself loose, swung up and, taking the reins of Gabriel's horse, started off along the road leading to the town.

3

No Chains for Shiloh

'Cowards die many times before their deaths — the valiant never taste of death but once!' eulogized Mayor Sam 'Shakespeare' Jones at one of the smallest funerals Durant had ever seen.

'And so it was with our dear brother and true friend, Ford Gabriel,' he continued after a dramatic pause. 'A brave man, a hero and guardian of the weak. Just as the good Samaritan halted by the wayside to lend succour to the man robbed and beaten by brigands, so did our good brother Ford come here to Durant to stay and help us. And now . . . '

A dramatic gesture towards the casket.

'And now he lies cold and dead, foully murdered by one unfit to touch his bootstraps. Oh, what a black day it is for us, my countrymen, as bloody treason triumphs over us!'

Heads nodded in sober agreement. Mayor Jones was elected year after year for two reasons. The failed Shakespearean actor turned storekeeper, with his tall figure and flowing mane, was the only man in the region who looked the way a real mayor should. And nobody could spill out the flowery words like Sam. So, for baptisms, burials, marriages and roof-raisings Shakespeare could be counted on to get up on skinny legs and hold forth. It didn't seem to matter if a lot of what he said might be pure drivel, just so long as it sounded right and caused the older women to dab at their eyes.

The reality regarding Gabriel was that, although not a likeable man, he had provided a measure of protection for this high country outpost in recent times. Most mourners today were less grieving than pondering what might befall them now the gunman was gone to meet his Maker.

None would deny that the brooding Gabriel alone had proven a formidable deterrent to anybody who might wish Durant harm, for whatever reason. And it was widely believed he'd prevented the ambitious Marcus Whitman from taking control there to further his political ambitions. Gabriel might have continued doing so indefinitely, had not Shiloh come to the high country.

What was never understood was Gabriel's reason for staying on. Why should a top gun hang his hat in Durant? And what could be the attraction of the shabby room at the Durant Hotel and the lousy meals at the Greasy Spoon eatery, when he could have been hiring his gun and living in high style in Denver or Virginia City?

Whatever the reason, none would know now. Not with Ford lying stiff and stark in the cheapest coffin the undertaker had been able to knock up for him, they wouldn't.

The voice of the wordy mayor droned on, drifting out over choking weeds and odd-angled headstones and across green slopes and sun-shimmering rooftops, faintly reaching the motionless figure leaning against a tree dragging reflectively on a freshly lighted cigar.

Shiloh inhaled and flicked ash from his cheroot as he idly studied the puffy clouds and watched how the breeze fingered the trees around the cemetery, as the remains were lowered into the grave.

He took another drag as mourners began filtering from the graveyard. Soon they were moving by his position upon the knoll, some making their way to horses and wagons but most passing on foot.

None seemed conscious of his presence until a knot of mourners including Shakespeare Jones came by. The preacher-mayor spotted him and stopped in his tracks.

'A great foulness has come upon this land!' he boomed, outrage inflating bony chest. 'Ahh, that just one amongst us possessed the courage to smite down this thing that so offends the eye! See you his pride in the dark and evil deed he has done! Witness if you will, his towering vanity. If there be justice a lightning bolt shall surely this instant smite him down!'

The mayor waited. No thunderbolt. He made to say more but a mourner silenced him with a warning finger, and he trudged off, still muttering.

Times like this, Shiloh seemed to drift within his mind. Killing gave him no joy or pride. But all his life he'd believed if a man was not prepared to fight then he should be ready to die. He derived no satisfaction from his victory here, yet knew if anyone should challenge him now he would shoot him down exactly as he had Gabriel.

That was how he lived, how he had been made.

He folded his arms and appeared relaxed as another group approached. Trailing in the wake of the mayor was the storekeeper and his wife, the bartender from the saloon with two large spinsterish-looking females. And the girl, Jill Flynn.

She was the daughter of the town blacksmith. No older than eighteen, she was slender, wide-eyed and pretty as four aces.

He supposed she too was afraid of him.

Yesterday when he'd ridden into the town proper with Gabriel's body across his saddle, he'd felt the town's fear. Yet the girl seemed unaffected. She had directed him to the undertaker-carpenter as calmly as if he was enquiring about the best place to eat.

He liked strong women.

'Look at him, brothers and sisters! See the lust in his eyes as he leers over our immaculate children. What — '

Somebody again attempted to silence the mayor, but he had an audience and felt safe in a crowd. 'Dirty butcher!' he yelled, forgetting his prose. 'Get back to whoever sent you here, killer!'

'When I'm ready . . . maybe,' Shiloh murmured to himself, eyes still upon the girl, who was moving on.

'Murder most foul!'

'Take it easy, Jones,' a man said. 'It was a fair fight, not a murder.'

'That's a dirty lie. No man could beat Fast Ford. He was the fastest of the fast.'

'He's played that tune once too often,' Shiloh said, replacing his hat and flicking a glance at Shakespeare's companions. 'Might be smart to move him on.'

The mayor opened his big mouth to say more, but was immediately seized by the arms and hurried off by men smarter than himself. Clint stared after them, then realized one of the passing group had fallen back.

He nodded gravely. 'Miss . . . ?'

'Perhaps you should leave?' Jill Flynn suggested. 'You've done what you came here to do. What can you gain by staying on?'

'Anybody ever tell you you're real pretty?'

He couldn't distract her. 'Won't you please go? There could be trouble. I know Ford was a killer, but he did have friends here — '

'Were you one of them?'

'No. But please let me finish. We saw too much killing while he was here, so surely the last thing we want is another killer taking his place.' A pause and a frown. 'You weren't sent here to stay, were you?'

'No. Just kill and ride out.' He spoke with calculated brutality now, trying to shake her composure. 'Our kind likes simple orders. We're not that clever, you know?'

He admired the way she simply returned his look gravely, standing there in full sunlight. And was taken completely off-guard when the old ache hit him. He thought of it as the 'High Lonesome' feeling . . . the sensation of total solitariness that came with his trade. It was an emotion that struck but rarely, yet always hit hard. He'd been alone all his days and believed it would be like that forever.

But he simply shrugged, flipped a bullet and caught it, and next moment the feeling was gone.

'Did that man send you here?' she asked after a silence.

'Who?'

'Marcus Whitman.'

'Never heard of him.'

Her eyes told him she knew he lied. He already knew many here believed he had come here on Whitman's orders. Everyone here seemed to fear the man from Denver. With Gabriel gone, Durant expected Whitman to return here eventually and and take up from where he'd been forced to quit several months earlier, with his aspirations to win this seat in the State Assembly seemingly left hanging.

He shrugged supple shoulders and thought, *What did he care?* And yet, somehow, he did.

He reckoned Gabriel had likely been much like himself, a professional born into the gun trade. Yet he still puzzled why the fast gun had quit the high-paying life to play nursemaid to a bunch of hicks up here for little more than his keep.

He sensed this curiosity was the reason he lingered. He wanted to figure that one out. Yet even now he could feel the trail pulling at him . . . the eternal lure of the next far horizon . . . the next showdown . . .

He moved down to the road with arms swinging freely, paused to touch hatbrim.

'See you when the grapes get right, pretty woman. You'll be cheered to know I'm leaving.'

He started off, but paused at the sound of quick steps behind. 'Mr Shiloh?'

He turned with a question in his eyes.

'I'd like to speak to you privately for a moment. Are you making for the livery?'

For just a moment he felt suspicion. But then he nodded in agreement. For there was no danger for him here. He'd erased it all when Fast Ford went down.

They moved on and were soon to be seen strolling along Main, raising eybrows. They made an eye-catching couple, Durant's prettiest girl in her sober Quaker-cloth dress walking at the side of the lithe gunslinger. Shiloh's hat hung down his back by the throat strap and the sun sheened his dark head of hair.

A big, bearded man with an angry red face suddenly appeared in the batwing doorway of the Busted Luck Saloon.

'Jilly!' shouted blacksmith Ben Flynn. 'Just what in the tarnal do you think you are doing?'

The girl paused. 'It's all right, Dad.'

'The hell it is!' The smithy stamped out on to the porch followed by several cronies. 'You just get on home, girl, and don't be flaunting yourself with the likes of this — '

Ben Flynn stopped mid-sentence as

Shiloh covered two quick steps to mount the porch before him.

'You were saying, mister?' His voice was cold. He knew how to scare people. 'You know, gunfighters aren't gentlemen yet most of us know better than to disrespect women. Now . . . you were saying?'

It was embarrassing to watch big Ben Flynn deflate before a man half his weight and inches shorter. Red-faced now, the man backed up, his support group quickly deserting him. 'Er, I guess I . . . well . . . '

Shiloh's easy smile came to his rescue.

'I can understand, mister,' he drawled softly. 'I wouldn't care for a daughter of mine to be seen with a gunman. But don't fret. She is safer with me than some here who look like they'd faint clear away at the first whiff of trouble.'

'You enjoyed doing that, didn't you?' the girl accused as they continued on, leaving her father chewing his beard in silence. 'You enjoy humiliating people and making them appear small just because of that stupid gun — as if that's anything to be proud of!'

'Don't bad-name gunspeed, miss,' he drawled, taking a cigar from his breast pocket and setting it between his teeth. 'Sometimes it's the only way you can tell the men from the boys in this life.'

They were approaching Cleever's Livery.

'I would think that would be the last thing I would judge anyone by.' She appeared to be calming some.

'I don't make the rules . . . just live by them.'

The livery was cool and gloomy and filled with the good smells of leather, oats and fresh hay. He jerked his saddle off the stall wall and moved away to saddle Two Bits. He was conscious of the girl's eyes upon him as he completed the familiar saddling chore. He led the animal out and began strapping on his warbag.

He had packed and readied for the trail earlier, having decided to quit

Durant directly after the funeral service. No sign of the liveryman. Shiloh figured the man was keeping low, probably scared like the rest of this town. He was sure of this, yet sensed Durant appeared even edgier than most places. He could imagine one huge sigh of relief when he disappeared.

That random thought somehow seemed to make what the girl said next even the more surprising. 'Mr Shiloh, must you leave?'

He stared. 'What?'

'Oh, I can understand how you're thinking after the things I've said. I meant them. But it was only after what happened with my father at the saloon that I sensed you might be able to help us. In fact I've become convinced you're possibly the only man who could.' She lifted her chin. 'That is why I'm swallowing my pride and asking you to stay.'

'Stay in Hicksville, USA? What the hell for?'

'To protect us.'

His frown deepened. 'From what?'

'Marcus Whitman, of course.'

'But I — '

'I know. You work for him. But he is a vile and vicious man who will stop at nothing to get what he wants, be it power, money ... even a woman. Before the council hired Ford Gabriel, we lived in constant fear of Whitman and his thugs, and that's how it will be again now Gabriel is gone.' She paused. 'Why are you staring that way?'

'Why? On account it was Whitman who sent me here, damnit!'

She appeared to take that in her stride.

'I'm not surprised. Well if one man can hire you why not others? You are a guman who rents his gun. Well, why not hire your gun to Durant to protect us?'

'Well, I'll be damned! Tell me, did you think this up all by yourself?'

'Yes. Will you consider the offer?'

'No chance.'

Her face fell. She was very pretty. But he tried not to think about that. Hire out to a bunch of hicks against a ruthless bastard like Whitman? A man would have to be loco!

She touched his arm. 'But why not? We could pay you.'

He shook his head. 'Look, what you need here is a gun who doesn't mind sitting around for months on end trying to look tough. Another Fast Ford, maybe. I couldn't stomach that for a start. And if I did I'd want big dinero, lady — '

'How much?'

'Damnit — '

'Fifty dollars a week? That's what the council was paying Ford.'

'Fifty? Try two hundred.'

'You know we could never afford that. But if I could appeal to your better nature — '

'Lady, I don't have a better nature.'

'Mr Shiloh, I realize Ford Gabriel was just a gunman for hire who didn't really care about us. Yet he did protect us. Marcus Whitman wants to take over everything here — expand our copper mine and suchlike. But, mainly, of course, in order that he might bully us into supporting him in the elections.'

'Look, lady — '

'I could take you to the cemetery and show you the graves of men who died here fighting Whitman's thugs and gunmen before we hired Gabriel. The moment Whitman learns Gabriel is gone he'll be back and it will all start again. But you could stop it. You could help us.'

'Why should I?'

'Because we need you.'

'Well, I'm sorry all to hell,' he snapped, swinging up, 'but you're asking the wrong man. And if this town figured you might be able to reach me with those green eyes and pretty hair, then they read me wrong!'

The gunfighter took a twisted pleasure in the tears he saw brimming in her eyes now. There had been times when a starving brat living in the sewers of a Virginia City winter had tears frozen to his eyes, and nobody to give a solitary damn.

'See you when the grapes get ripe,' he said coldly, and kicked Two Bits away.

In brilliant sunshine, towners still in their church clothes stepped down into the street to watch him ride out. Somebody shouted a curse and an urchin flung a pebble but the gunfighter's eyes remained fixed upon the way ahead.

A sneer flickered at the edge of Clint Shiloh's mind as Two Bits danced through the summer dust along the curving trail below Boot Hill.

So long, Fast Ford! I hope it was worth it, fighting for a bunch of yellow towners just for peanuts and a hole six feet deep and six long. That would never be enough for Clint Shiloh!

4

Shoot-out At Sweet Creek

The party was less than a half-day's ride out along the climbing trail from Sweet Creek before Marcus Whitman confided in his henchmen that his pending payoff for Clint Shiloh had, what he termed, a 'Whitman twist' to it.

By the time he'd made his plans clear, even the brutish Durkin appeared uneasy. In truth, squatting by the fire they'd built to brew coffee while the horses grazed and rested in a grassy swale, the outsized gunman almost gagged on the Arbuckles he was drinking. This set him off coughing, leaving it to runty little Cut Woodtsock to do the protesting.

'Kill Shiloh, you say, boss? What in hell for?'

It was the obvious question, considering the situation. For Whitman had been an impatient exile from the War God Hills electorate, where he was already overdue to mount his campaign for the legislature, due principally to the menacing gun-guardianship of Ford Gabriel.

Of course, during that time he'd been neither idle nor passive. The contrary, in fact. Scarce anybody realized that Whitman — this candidate for high office — had in fact secretly dispatched no less than three guns for hire up to the high country on different occasions with the specific task of eliminating Fast Ford.

The result had been two gunmen shot up and the fate of the third marked only by Whitman's receipt of a postal box containing the third man's blood-stained hat.

'But fourth time lucky,' as he'd taken to reassuring his henchmen of late. He'd had a good feeling after agreeing to meet Clint Shiloh's exorbitant fee to take Durant's gunman down. Already the newspapers back in Denver were trumpeting the front page news of Gabriel's death in a gun duel, while speculating at length upon the expected political consequences.

Whitman had brooked no delay in finalizing his long-delayed plans to return to the high valley, now perceived as safe. Nobody was surprised by this considering the political situation, and the looming election date. But what came as unexpected and even alarming news to his gunhands was Whitman's calm revelation that his 'reward' to the man who'd brought Fast Ford down, would not be the extra $300 cash as promised, but rather a ticket to Boot Hill.

They were stunned into momentary silence. Surely he must be joking?

Marcus Whitman was deadly serious.

'Let me explain, gentlemen,' he told them in his patronizing way. 'You may or may not be aware that the elections for the State Assembly are due to be held at the end of this month.'

Jack Curran, who hadn't even seen

the State Assembly, much less could understand what its function might be, stared blankly across at fat Luke Harris, who appeared equally puzzled.

Their reactions revealed the pair as newcomers to this quarter of the big country west of the Mississippi. But both Woodstock and Durkin had been handling Whitman's dirty work for some time, and fully understood both the workings of the legislature and their employer's ambitions to sit with his elected peers in that big governmental chamber in Denver by month's end.

But up until that moment neither man had heard any hint of taking the formidable Shiloh out of the game. In truth it sounded loco, doubly so in light of the fact that Shiloh had done such a professional job in taking Ford Gabriel out of the game. Small wonder the pair were suddenly leaning forward and playing close attention to whatever might be coming up next.

Whitman didn't disappoint.

'To win election to the legislature,

gentlemen, a candidate in Colorado needs to receive a certain number of votes lodged by specifically registered landowners in his chosen electorate. That is, ranchers of substance and property who own land of at least the size of a full section. At the moment the War God Hills region is carved up into dozens of single or double-section spreads, each one of which represents a citizen who is entitled to vote either for me or my opponent, Sam Worth of Taloga. Savvy?'

Heads nodded. Whitman took a pull on his cigar and continued.

'Now that I'm finally rid of Gabriel up there, I'm embarking on a campaign to win over the high-valley ranchers and convince them to think and vote my way . . . '

Here he paused to stare at each hardcase in turn. When he spoke, again, his words came as flat and hard as a rifle shot. 'And, as I just said, rid myself of Shiloh at the same time.'

They stared. They knew what he was

saying, still didn't understand why. 'What — ?' Durkin began uneasily, but was cut off.

'Common sense, really,' Whitman stated flatly. 'You see, Shiloh has outlived his usefulness to me. Sure, I'll grant he handled the Gabriel job expertly. Smooth as silk, in truth. But as I will now be working overtime to regain the voters' respect and trust before voting day, I can't have people running round claiming Shiloh shot Gabriel on my orders . . . or even risk Shiloh maybe blabbing about it to the wrong people at the wrong time. Who knows?'

He paused to touch a vesta to a fresh stogie.

'From here on in I have to be seen as the War God voters' best friend. But I've got to erase all suspicion that I had Gabriel eliminated. And what better way to prove that than by blasting the man who shot their protector down . . . so avenging 'poor' Ford? *Compre* now?'

Heads nodded. Finally they understood. Which wasn't the same as saying they liked it. The term, 'Blasting Shiloh' seemed loaded with uncertainties.

'Well, I guess the way you put it . . . it's gotta be done, boss man,' Woodstock said at length.

It was no ringing endorsement. But that didn't faze Whitman. This was his game for high stakes, and he was the one calling the shots. Like always.

'Smart man.' Whitman ashed his cigar. 'But how do we go about getting rid of him — do I hear you ask?'

'Shiloh's chain lightning with that .45, boss,' Curran felt obliged to point out. 'Mebbe as fast as they come — '

'And no fool neither,' observed Durkin, massaging his heavy jaw. 'You sure there ain't a simpler way, boss? I mean, mebbe — '

'Shiloh is just another gun punk, nothing more and nothing less!' No fancy words or crafty smiles now. Whitman was talking gun-barrel straight, at last. 'I always contend if you hire any man to kill for you, the day might come when he might be tempted by the dollar to spill his guts to the wrong people. Particularly when I'm Senator Whitman, I just couldn't afford to let that happen.'

Heads nodded, yet still without enthusiasm.

But Whitman remained resolute.

'That's one reason I'll see him dead,' he continued briskly, emptying the dregs of his coffee into the fire. 'The lesser of two, in truth. That's due to the fact that, no matter what I say, some folks here will go on believing I had Shiloh gun Gabriel to clear the path for my return to the high country and start charming the voters again. But reckon on this. What if I really was innocent of that 'crime?' And what if I was so outraged by Shiloh killing Gabriel that I felt bound by conscience to avenge the man's death crime?'

He paused. He could see they were impressed now.

Cut Woodstock was first to speak. 'Y'know, that's pretty slick thinking, boss. Sneaky and tricky, maybe, but clever.'

'A perfect plan,' Whitman insisted. 'Even if tough on Shiloh to be offered up as the sacrificial lamb on the altar of my larger plan . . . '

He paused and smiled. He liked the way he'd put that.

'He ain't no kind of lamb,' stubborn Durkin insisted. 'Lots of folks reckoned Gabriel couldn't be beat. Yet Shiloh stepped on him like a bug. Taking him down ain't gonna be any kind of cinch.'

The silence that descended was intended to give Whitman time maybe to think twice. It didn't work that way. Suddenly he was on his feet facing them, as proddy and commanding and ruthless as they'd ever seen him.

'We're taking him out!' he rapped. 'Anybody who doesn't like it, there's the door!'

They traded looks. After an uncertain moment, lethal Woodstock managed a half-smile. Durkin glanced around, then nodded his big head, which seemed to encourage Curran and Harris. Suddenly all four were drawing strength from one another as much as from Whitman's words, and found themselves wondering what they'd been fretting about.

For the numbers, after all, would be four to one.

'You're right, boss man,' Harris spoke up confidently. He shrugged and put on a tough grin. 'So, how's it going to be done?'

Whitman lit a cigar and told them.

★ ★ ★

Sometimes the ghosts didn't trouble him for months on end. Yet they were with him in strength tonight, sinister shades from the past seemingly ghosting by amongst the bright lights and swirling tobacco smoke of the Devilrider Saloon.

In turn a pensive Shiloh imagined himself visited by the shades of Colorado Brown, Fast Jim Bowner and

75

Sam Hackenburn, all men who'd faced him, now all gone. Then he sensed the dark spirit of the late Bat Dongin who'd left him with a jagged scar across his ribcage where the bullet had missed his heart by an inch back in those days before he'd fully mastered his craft.

He attempted to lift his mood by erasing the dead from his mind and concentrated instead on the many he'd permitted to live — a Godlike role that mostly only gunslingers and judges ever got to play.

He recalled young Billy Moore from Denver who'd actually bullet-creased his shoulder with his lightning draw. In response Shiloh simply shot the cutter out of the kid's fist and told him to go on home and have his momma wipe his nose . . .

Then there was Dooley Rhodes, the man they called Dusty . . . Sidewinder Smith . . . the Black brothers. All gun heroes who had challenged him over the years, yet most were still breathing and maybe still working at the gun trade for all he knew. None owed their lives to luck, but rather to him. He'd proven often you didn't always have to kill. Not if you were fast enough to get the jump, then send them off to consider taking up something they might really excel at. Like farming or bee-keeping, maybe.

And all this time, he was watching the door for Whitman to show. He raised a glass to his reflection in the back-bar mirror glass, and drank his whiskey down.

It was eight o'clock on a Saturday night and the Devilrider was generating enough racket for a place twice its size. The professor was at his piano banging out a noisy song, and the girls were laughing as they danced with the wild cowboys down from the hills.

Sweet Creek's Devilrider was the only saloon in twenty miles that boasted a dance floor. Spittoons gleamed dully beneath lamps that swayed to the vibration of stomping feet. The sawdust scattered over the boards was pink and damp.

Shiloh ordered another and tapped his fingertips on the bar in time with the music.

The steady beat kept the figures whirling and the yellow light which spilled over them illuminated the empty space wary drinkers had left around him at the bar. Poker chips clattered, hard money clinked, whiskey bottles were slammed down upon the bartop. And every now and then, somebody whispered to a new arrival, 'That's him! That's Clint Shiloh!'

And not one of them asked dumbly, 'Who's he?' All knew, even those sighting him for the first time. His name was on everybody's lips as the man who'd shot Ford Gabriel down in the high country.

So — *Adios*, Fast Ford! Welcome your conqueror! And let's have another to celebrate the occasion!

Sweet Creek was that kind of town, rough, uncaring yet viciously envious of its successful rancher neighbours fifteen miles up-country on War God Hill. Or Silvertail County, as they labelled it.

Nothing 'silvertailed' about Sweet Creek. Down here it was loose women, ragged shirt-tails, drunken brawling and rowdy and rollicking Saturday nights. Who cared about high country snobs who shaved most days and even boasted their own lousy church? Not us, for sure.

There was constant surging movement in the long, low-ceilinged room which contained ten round tables, forty wooden chairs, six overhead tallow lamps and the all-important long bar.

Talk shuttled through smoky air, broken by sudden male laughter and the shriller cries of the women. All the smells were heavy: sweat, beer, tallow, perfume, cloves, grease, leather, horse scents.

But in his mind now the gunfighter was back in the high Celindas where he'd gone fishing for a few days after his gun work.

He'd thrown up a little lean-to on the stony bank of a trout stream. He fished, walked, hunted and dreamed with nobody but Two Bits, the uncaring peaks and his own thoughts for company. Strange, but the ghosts never seemed to trouble him when he was alone. Only at times like this when there was noise and people did the shades of the dead make themselves felt to the man of the gun.

Time was when the ghosts bothered him. Not any more. Soon, he knew, the image of Ford Gabriel would also fade. The dead were like old friends now, some of them. For weren't they all brothers of the gun? And most had died bravely. Which could never be said of those back-shooters and sidewinders, for whom any man who rode as high as himself must be forever watchful.

Whatever their shortcomings, all those he'd faced had gone like men, gun in hand and defiance in the eye. Lived and died like men. There was much to be said for that . . .

'You're getting serious again, Shiloh . . . '

He shook his head to banish the images and found they were all still dancing, singing and brawling . . . and his glass was empty again.

Another?

That sounded great. It was just too bad he'd had his last for this night. He felt good, yet knew that just one more shot might rob him of that lethal edge which no gunfighter could ever risk losing. Though there seemed little prospect of bumping into another Ford Gabriel down here, a man could never be sure.

Nobody had encroached on his elbow room for quite a time, when the percentage girl with a flower in her hair approached.

'Buy me a drink, mister?'

'Beat it.'

She stayed put. She was a slim child-woman with a red wound of a mouth and over-bright eyes that told him she was bucked up on liquor. She studied him insolently, her gaze playing over his unlined cheeks, straight nose, black dash of a moustache.

She swayed a little. 'Hell! You really the feller that's got them all walking on air? You ain't scarce older than me.'

He knew he should send her on her way. Instead he merely stared at her. She looked like a child, a lost child. His enemies claimed Clint Shiloh was a man without compassion, yet he had always felt something for lost children, even a shop-worn, manhandled adult child like this.

He said gently, 'I can't buy you a drink. I'm busy. I'm expecting somebody.'

That was the truth. He was expecting Whitman. She thought he was lying. But she didn't seem to care one way or another. 'You look just like my brother, Tommy,' she declared, drawing closer. 'It's true. Saloon girls aren't supposed to have kinfolk and suchlike. Well, I got me a real brother and he looks just like you.' Her eyes turned sad. 'Fine looking feller he is too . . . '

He smiled — the man of the gun was actually smiling at a shop-soiled saloon angel when it happened. The batwings swung inwards and Marcus Whitman strode in trailed by his flankers from Tincup.

'Better move on, sweetheart,' Shiloh murmured. 'Here comes the feller I'm expecting.'

The girl turned to blink at the new arrivals who had halted just inside the swinging doors, customers respectfully moving back to give them space.

'Oh, him!' she snorted. 'You are waiting for him? In that case I'll leave you to it. I never did have any time for that Whitman, and that goes double after this afternoon . . . '

She was moving off on unsteady feet when Shiloh reached out and grabbed her by the arm.

'Just a minute,' he said. 'You're saying Whitman was here earlier?'

'Sure was. And he spoke to me like dirt, just like he used to do when he was bossing folks about here before.

Said I was listening in to a private talk between him and Ace Burke. How the hell did I know it was private?'

'Which one is Burke?'

She indicated a tall man in a flashy brown jacket and bed-of-flowers vest seated at a poker layout nearby.

'That's Ace. Say, who's he staring at that way anyway? You or me? I'm not seeing any too well tonight.'

Ace Burke was staring directly at Shiloh. Or was, until Shiloh chanced to catch his eye. Then he dropped his gaze quickly. Too quickly.

The back of Shiloh's neck tingled. He'd been waiting here for Whitman to receive the balance of his fee for the gun job. That should be simple enough. But why this sudden feeling that caused him to reach down to ensure his six-gun was in place and loose in its holster?

He didn't know ... but for a gunfighter there could always be vague signs, signals or hunches it never paid to disregard.

Unhurriedly, he pressed a five-dollar bill into the girl's hand, silenced her with a finger to her lips, then gave her a gentle shove that set her tottering off in search of someone who didn't act so strange.

He knew Whitman had arrived in town earlier today, as expected. But that sharp glance between Whitman and Burke now touched off a faint alarm bell of warning.

How come Whitman had sought that flash bastard out earlier, yet not looked him up?

He was alert as Whitman now turned and came towards him. The tall man's smoothly shaven features were blank. But Durkin, Harris and Curran weren't the good actors their employer was. Shiloh could feel their tension like heat coming off a branding iron.

Trouble hung in the smoky air of the Devilrider Saloon. Big trouble.

But why?

* * *

Shiloh appeared the most relaxed man in the saloon as Whitman approached him confidently to shake his hand. He congratulated him warmly on the Gabriel job then insisted on treating him to the best drink in the house.

Clint managed a faint smile even though conscious that Whitman appeared taut as a coiled spring behind his mask of affability. Nor did he fail to note that Durkin and the others had fanned out in a wide semi-circle as they slowly emerged from the crowd.

He stared into Whitman's face and felt a prickle down his spine at what he saw there, suddenly seemed to realize he was confronting a man both far cleverer and more treacherous than he'd understood before.

Smoothly, unnoticed by the other, his hand slid towards his gunbutt . . .

Whatever Whitman was hatching here tonight — and every danger-honed sense warned that something was surely brewing — he was ready. Of course, the back of his mind reasoned, he could be wrong. Maybe Whitman simply had something weighty on his mind that was responsible for that strange look in his eye? Then again, being such a vain son of a bitch, he might feel he had the right to talk down to him to make himself appear big in the eyes of the mob, to be seen riding rough-house over a gunfighter.

Or could it be something one hell of a lot more?

And his gunfighter's pride was pricked as he thought, *Think twice, big man. This is Clint Shiloh you're dealing with, not some fifth-rater like Cantrell* . . .

At the end of a brief conversation, Whitman was suddenly called away by Cut Woodstock. He smiled to excuse himself, then quickly merged with the crowd. Shiloh's gaze followed his every step. Suddenly Whitman propped and turned, touching a white silk handkerchief to his brow.

If that was not a signal then Shiloh had never seen one.

He drew and fired in one fluent motion as Curran's .45 leapt into his hand behind the cover of an unsuspecting drinker. The hardcase stopped the bullet in the shoulder and bystanders screamed as he toppled to the boards, convulsing in agony.

As the yelling rose above the thunder of the gunshot, Shiloh was moving fast. He swung his Colt barrel to smash against the skull of a man blocking his eyeline. He shouldered the sagging body aside then pivoted to kick the mean-faced legs out from under Luke Harris, and caved the man's face in with his elbow on his way to the floor.

And every move was so blindingly swift few amongst the mob fully realized what they were seeing.

In moments, the saloon was in chaotic upheaval with drinkers crashing blindly into one another as they attempted to escape this sudden madness of screaming women and exploding six-guns.

And low down now at the heart of the turmoil, a crouching figure was lining up the nearest of the big drop lights with a smoking six-shooter . . .

Just four rapid-fire shots saw every blue-tinted lamp explode and shower glass and oil over the chaotic scene below. In almost total darkness now, pandemonium reigned with people rushing every which way only to crash blindly into others gripped by the same sense of panic. They howled and cursed and collided like blind beasts as they milled in the darkness, with a cool Shiloh virtually the only one who knew what he was doing and where he was headed.

For this was far from his first saloon ruckus.

Knowing just where he was going, his crouching figure bobbed and jinked its way nimbly through the mass of seething humanity with his gaze fixed unwaveringly upon the skinny chink of light the side door was letting in from the street.

And every moment he was chain-lightning fast and ready to kick, punch, shove or pistol-whip anybody who might get in his way.

Within moments he was outside in the sweet night air with nothing worse than scratches, and his eyes watering from kerosene smoke.

Heading for the hitch-rail close by, where Two Bits waited nervously, he shot a glance back over his shoulder. No sign of the saloon catching fire as yet. Even if it had done, he wouldn't be able to help. Not with Whitman howling for his blood, he wouldn't.

And he thought fiercely . . . Whitman! He realized he'd never fully trusted that high-stepping son of a whore. Now he knew why.

He had snapped his horse's lines free when a six-gun bellowed from close by and a fierce pain raked the side of his head.

He was knocked down, scarce able to believe he'd been shot. Staggering erect with vision blurring, he realized the bullet had not come from the Devil-rider but rather from the darkened porch of the haberdashery in back of the hitch-rack.

'Got you, you firebuggin' bastard!' a drunken voice roared, then another bullet missed him by at least one hundred feet.

He couldn't believe it. He'd survived the madness inside unscathed, yet now some staggering wino flukes him!

He was angry enough to shoot back, yet didn't. Instead he came fully erect to touch off a single shot, placing it within a hair's breadth of the reeling figure who howled in sudden panic and dived blindly for cover.

Shiloh might have cursed had he the breath. He didn't. Instead he vaulted into the saddle and raked with spur to go hammering away.

Blood leaked down from the side of his head.

He ignored the pain and fought the dimness until within the space of a minute he was clear of Sweet Creek and making instinctively north for the high country. They mightn't care for him up there, but at least the bastards weren't trying to kill him. He ripped out a shirtsleeve to staunch the blood, yet continued to bleed. Like a wounded lobo wolf his one thought was to reach the War God Hills and lie up until whole again.

Instinct saw him steer Two Bits for the the pass that led to the high Celindas. Maybe he could make it to that camp he'd fixed up high in the hills beyond Durant . . . 'Got to make it,' he panted in time with the drumming hoofbeats. He could not understand why bright moonlight was fading into darkness . . .

5

Here Comes the Judge

The flaked gold lettering on the rusted iron gate still read 'Judge Vernon Clutterloe', even though it was now some years since Clutterloe's name had been struck from the records of Justices of the Peace for drunkenness and incompetence.

'The Judge', as he was still known around squalid Sweet Creek, was an avid dabbler in politics, the shadier the better. He had friends in high places despite a deeply tarnished reputation. He could still boast some solid connections, and his background and experience made him a valuable ally for any man with high ambitions and a quiet conscience.

With Assembly elections upcoming on the frontier, the judge was more active than usual these days.

It was almost nine when the dapper figure in the derby hat arrived at the judge's house on Foster Street. Like the judge himself, the house had seen better days. It was a dilapidated structure with towering gateposts of terracotta that reared like a giant's fingerbones out of a wilderness of overgrown flower beds and under-growth.

Whitman gave a jerk on the bell rope and from deep in the house came a faint jingle. Presently heavy footsteps sounded and the judge's manservant answered the door then showed the visitor into the study.

Clutterloe was drinking his breakfast in back. He was a paunchy wreck of a man on skinny legs with dirty grey hair. The ends of his moustache curled upwards, waxed into needle points. Upon entering the study, he surveyed his visitor whom he knew had been involved in the shoot-out at the Devil-rider, a wild incident which had all

Clearwater County chattering that day.

'Care for a brandy, Whitman?' Clutterloe offered, casually, waving his bottle of liquid breakfast.

'No.' Whitman was not a drinker at the best of times, and today was definitely not one of those.

The judge shrugged, waved him to a chair, then rested a buttock on a corner of his desk. 'Well, sir, you made a fine mess of things last night I hear tell?'

Owing to the fact that Whitman was seeking Clutterloe out to help further his political fortunes, as he had done in the past, he supposed that entitled the judge some right to criticize. But the visitor was still noticeably terse as he proceeded to explain exactly what had occurred at the saloon, and why. The judge did not appear quite so critical by the time he was through.

'Hmm . . . I rather feel your decision to rid yourself of Shiloh in order that by so doing you might represent yourself to the townsfolk of Durant as both protector and avenger, while silencing a possible talker at the same time, seems a sound one. But the hell-bent way you went about it, man . . . '

'There was no other way as I saw it.'

'No other way than going after a gunman in a crowded saloon? Come now, man!'

Whitman looked petulant.

'I wanted it done quick and in public so the whole damned county would know I was back and intent on proving I had nothing to do with the Gabriel affair.' He shook his sleek head. 'But that bastard is faster even than I figured. I believe he was hit, but there's still no sign of him . . . '

His voice trailed away. He was a man playing for high stakes in the always turbulent world of frontier politics.

'So, what's your position now?' the judge asked bluntly.

'I don't want that gunfighter on the loose with a score to settle . . . the big stakes I'll be playing for in the War Gods.' Whitman looked up, his expression brightening. 'But Shiloh was hit.

Some idiot drunk on the street got excited by all the uproar, took a potshot and drilled him, they say.'

'Well, that's better. So, where is he now?'

'Gone.'

'Gone? I thought you said — ?'

'I said he was hit, is all. Some on the street said it looked bad, others weren't sure.'

The judge had no sympathy. The two had worked together on several shady deals over time, and the judge was part of Whitman's scheme to carry the Hills in the upcoming election. The judge started in summarizing the situation, but his visitor cut him off.

'I didn't come here to be lectured, you damned old fraud.'

The judge studied his man, then relaxed some. 'All right, all right, calm down, Marcus. What's done is done.'

He slid off his desk, moved around to his chair and sat. He looked like a gargoyle, yet a clever one. He spoke softly. 'Why did you come to visit me,

Marcus? I mean . . . the real reason?'

'To discuss my future plans and my next move in light of last night, of course. You don't think I enjoy your company, do you?'

This was typical Whitman. Whenever uncertain, attack.

'What do you have in mind?'

Whitman leaned forward intently. 'Well, nobody knows for sure I caused the riot last night, though there's any amount of speculation going on.'

'I can imagine why.'

'The hell with that! I'm here for an opinion. Figure: in light of last night, do you believe I ruined my prospects of winning over Durant and the War God Hills electorate with this shoot-up?'

Crafty eyes set deep in wrinkles that were as deep as canyons, surveyed Whitman for a long moment.

Then, 'Perhaps not, Marcus. That is, if you are prepared to outlay some hard cash in order to, shall we say . . . silence the damaging talk and to oil the wheels?'

'What wheels?'

The judge straightened and talked fast.

'Blakely, editor of the *Chronicle*, is a so-called idealist. It costs serious money to persuade high-minded hypocrites like him to do what they are meant to do — namely, assist men like you and me whenever we might need it.'

'Keep talking.'

'Enough hard cash placed there will ensure that your version of how a mad-dog gunman ran amok and your people merely intervened to protect honest citizens, hits the front pages. For an extra two hundred I will personally pen an editorial damning this gunslinger while lauding you to the skies. I still have considerable influence hereabouts, regardless of my disbarment.'

Whitman was silent for a minute. He was considering. Suddenly, he felt brighter. Maybe he'd been impetuous last night — could even have been guilty of faulty judgement. But a good fighter always rolled with the punches, he told himself. And if last night had been bad, then at least his plan to rid himself of Gabriel was an outstanding success.

And, looking on the brighter side of last night — Shiloh could well be dead, lying in a mountain gully-wash some place with a drunk's slug in him.

And he thought: *Winners never quit and quitters never win!*

'OK, goddamnit!' he said briskly. 'We've got a deal. Just make sure you get results. I need the press and the local council bosses and businessmen all behind me down here as well as on War God. I'm giving you extra so you can grease the palms, and you had better, or — '

His voice cut off. Old Clutterloe's look was half smile, half grimace.

'Or what, mister? You were about to make a threat, weren't you? Certainly you were, as that is your nature. You're really just a dog wolf under that nifty suit, Whitman. But don't fret, I won't broadcast that fact. You just keep the money coming and I'll see you wind up in the State Assembly or my name isn't — '

He broke off. Whitman had what he'd come for and was gone, a man in a hurry.

★   ★   ★

On the street again. Whitman rammed both hand into his coat pockets and stood staring up at the hill country with smoke trailing from the cigar clamped between his teeth.

The War God Hills, vast and verdant were yet still at best half-civilized. For too long he'd been denied access up there due to several factors, prime amongst which had been the presence of Gabriel.

Over a period of time Whitman had dispatched several hardcases to the high country to rid himself of Gabriel, only to have them either disappear or arrive back in a coffin.

But Shiloh had finally opened the

gates again and there was nothing to prevent his returning up there to restate his claim on that all-important seat by convincing every voter in the War God Hills he was the man best qualified to represent the region in the Assembly.

He decided he would start up there immediately. But not without protection.

A short time later found him standing upon the main street gallery of Doc Talbot's three-bed hospital where Durkin had gone to get patched up overnight.

He was relieved when his gunman appeared with Talbot, showing nothing worse than a strapped leg and a limp.

'You do good work, Doc,' he assured the runty medico, oozing a politico's bogus charm. He nodded at his gunman, then added. 'How much?'

'Five will cover it, Mr Whitman.'

'Here's twenty.'

'How come?'

'I know more people were hurt in the shoot-up man. That's to cover their expenses as well . . . and just let them know Marcus Whitman wishes them well.'

'You know, some folks say harsh things about you, Mr Whitman. But for me, you are all right, damned if you're not.'

'Amazing what a little bit of the folding stuff can do, eh, boss?' tough Durkin grinned as they walked off. 'Just afore you showed up, that sawbones was telling me you touched off the gun ruckus. Yet a few bucks . . . and suddenly he thinks you're just swell.'

Before Whitman could respond he sighted a bunch of weary horsemen slowly turning into the main street. They were locals he'd paid to ride out and hunt for Shiloh in the wake of the shoot-out. Hard men who knew what was expected of them. His eyes searched hopefully for a body draped over a horse, but the party was plainly returning empty-handed.

'Looked all over, but no luck, Mr Whitman,' reported the leader of the bunch, drawing up. 'Sorry . . . '

'What do you really think, Durkin?' Whitman murmured as they watched the weary horsemen ride off for the livery. 'Do you think Shiloh might be dead?'

'Well, I never seen that drunk shoot him. But I did glimpse Shiloh galloping off, and he was sure weaving in the saddle.' He paused, nodded. 'Head wound. Uh-huh, if I was to guess I'd say he's either dead or dying by this.'

'Sounds good to me. OK, go round up the boys. Tell them we're leaving in an hour.'

'Right, boss. Er . . . where for?'

'For the War God Hills, of course. Gabriel's gone and Shiloh's likely gone, so I'm announcing it's electioneering time up there, mister. Get moving!'

The man strode off and Whitman took a deep drag of his cigar. It was a long time since tobacco had tasted quite so good.

6

Gunman in Town

It was early morning when Clint Shiloh stirred to the sound of voices raised in argument beyond the open window. Instantly aware of a pounding head, he opened his eyes cautiously to see Jilly Flynn standing by the end of the bed.

He blinked painfully as she smiled, then lifted his hand to the side of his head to touch heavy bandaging. For a moment he experienced blurred recollections of guns going off, wild shouting, and galloping furiously through the night. He frowned at the window as the sound of voices floated up from below.

'I tell you it just ain't right, Ben Flynn, you folks giving help and shelter to that dirty gunman. We had a confab about it at the saloon and we agreed that somebody ought to stand up and tell you just what we think — '

'Hold it right there, Joe Watson,' a deeper voice cut in. 'Are we Christians and civilized folk up here or ain't we?'

'Of course we are, Ben. Hell! I get down on me knees every night. But this . . . this here gunslinger, he's neither Christian nor civilized iffen you ask me. And we just don't reckon you should be — '

That was as much as the listener heard, as with a testy imprecation, the girl went to the window and banged the heel of her hand against the sill.

'Dad, Mr Haggin, will you kindly go argue someplace else? You're disturbing my patient!'

Shiloh raised himself on one elbow as the girl returned to his bedside. Her cheeks were flushed yet she managed a reassuring nod. Gazing past her at the window he glimpsed a lofty stand of sentinel pines, a cabin roof, and realized he was actually back in Durant in the high country. And wondered,

How in hell did I get here?

'How do you feel?' Her tone was brisk and matter-of-fact, as though she was accustomed to nursing shot-up gunmen every day of the week.

'Hungry,' he replied.

'That's a good sign.' Straightening his covers. 'I'll go fix some soup.'

Shiloh licked dry lips. 'No, hold on. First, some questions. Like, what am I doing here and how in tarnation did I get to be here — ?'

'Soup first,' she cut in. 'Then we'll check your dressing. We'll talk after that. Perhaps.'

Bossy, he thought. A mind of her own. And yet, he suspected, one damn fine nurse. His head felt good, considering. He'd been shot often enough to realize he might have been killed. It felt as if he'd lost plenty blood and he didn't need anybody to convince him he'd had a perilously close shave.

He was feeling stronger by the minute by the time she returned. Somehow he knew the soup would prove to be just great, which it was. He was feeling more like the old Clint Shiloh as Jilly Flynn attended to his bandages. She was all brisk efficiency as she cleansed his wound with brine, then strapped him up again.

And he thought: *One more close call, gunfighter! You've diced with Death again, and survived. But surely the odds must be shortening? It stands to reason that if you keep getting shot then the slug with your name on it must be clicking onwards around the gun chamber until it comes directly beneath the falling hammer* . . .

Jilly had barely finished when her father entered the room. Durant's smithy wore a blue flannel shirt unbuttoned to reveal a hairy, sweating chest. Plainly he'd been at work at the anvil already. The big man rested hands on hips and stood studying the gunfighter with little showing in his face.

Then, 'Reckon you're going to make it?'

Shiloh was equally laconic. 'Could do.' But his next words were difficult to get out. 'Thanks to you folks . . . that is.' In his world, the words 'thanks' or 'sorry' didn't really exist.

'You can thank Jilly for that,' Flynn declared. 'She sat with you most of the night. All I did was tote you up after Coley Wilkes stumbled across you lying down on a side trail leaking like a sieve.'

Shiloh was beginning to patch things together in his mind. 'I got this far? I don't remember. How long had I been out to it?'

'Couple of hours, we figured,' the blacksmith supplied. 'You'd leaked plenty blood. Doc says you've got mild concussion and loss of blood. But I suppose that's nothing to someone like you?'

He let that last remark slide on by.

He frowned. He had been that long unconscious and helpless? That very notion chilled him. About all he remembered was pain, weird dreams, and occasionally soft hands.

'So,' he grunted, flexing his arms and sitting up straighter, the strength really beginning to flood back now. 'How about Two Bits?'

'At the livery,' the blacksmith supplied. 'Far as we could figure that animal must have been standing watch over you a couple of hours afore Wilkes sighted him. You got a good animal there, Shiloh.'

The man's tone suggested he might have added; 'A man like you don't deserve a horse like that.' But Shiloh couldn't care less. He was fully armoured against contempt for his profession. But one thing he was not accustomed to was being beholden to folks. He was still puzzling over what they'd done for him when the father had lighted his pipe and left.

'Why . . . you're wondering?' Jilly guessed as though reading his thoughts, perching now on the corner of the bed. 'I know that's what must be on your mind right now. Well, we could hardly leave you out there on the trail to bleed

110

to death, now could we?'

'But . . . but you know what I am, what happened here before. I guess I'm used to people hating me, sure as shooting, not helping me out any.'

Her expression turned grave. 'Perhaps there's too much hate in the world. Mr Shiloh. I guess that's how most folks up here in Durant feel, leastways.'

His eyes narrowed suspiciously. 'You telling me you high-country people are different from other folks?'

'You appear to have a poor opinion of people in general.'

'I know it's a dog-eat-dog world,' he said with conviction. 'And I know nobody does nothing for nobody unless they've got an angle. What's yours?'

She rose gracefully. 'You don't trust anybody, do you?'

'Nobody trusts me, that's for sure.'

'Perhaps you never give people a chance?'

'Look — '

'No, no more talk. You must rest.'

111

'I've rested enough, bright-eyes.'

'My name is Jilly. And you are going to rest some more.'

Ignoring his protests she moved to the windows and drew the curtains. He swore softly as she went out, closing the door behind her. And yet he was half-grinning as he rested his head upon plumped-up pillows. He admired girls that you could not bully or bluff. Besides, his bullet crease was beginning to act up some again. But he steeled himself against the pain and was seriously considering swinging his feet to the floor when he felt his eyelids treacherously half-close.

It was the last thing he remembered, and next thing he knew, dusk shadows were silently filling his room.

He'd slept all day!

★ ★ ★

The following morning his nurse found she couldn't boss him any longer. Before breakfast he'd found the strength to get up, dress swiftly then circle the house a dozen times, growing stronger with each circuit.

He'd always been a fast healer. In his trade you had to be. You never knew when someone with a grudge, or maybe a contract with your name on it nestled snug in his hip pocket, might show up with a six-shooter in each hand.

The Colt was now buckled round his hips again within fingertip reach. Over breakfast, he kept watch on the town from the windows. He saw men arrive with horses for Ben Flynn to work on. Folks passed by, mostly either horse-backing or buggy-riding. Everywhere here you were made conscious of the huge distinction between lowland Sweet Creek and these prosperous farming and grazelands of the War God Hills.

The rural quiet of the large and solid-looking town was also in violent contrast to what he'd experienced at Sweet Creek.

Suddenly, he found himself reliving that night on the flatlands, was able to conjure up clearer recollections of running for his horse, a brutal blow to the side of the head, followed by a succession of fragmented images of the swift horse carrying him north into the high country below flickering black trees . . . an ever-intensifying dizziness in the cage of his skull.

Then blackness.

He flexed supple fingers and hefted his coffee mug. He realized he'd made enemies and scared folks here when he'd come after Gabriel, yet out there on the streets now there was no sign of anger or hostility as folks passed by the house. He sensed, rather than knew, that the blacksmith and his family stood high in this man's town, and if they were prepared to take him in then it seemed the town was ready to accept it.

Back to Sweet Creek. Why had Whitman tried to kill him? Knowing the man's reputation, he supposed he was hardly surprised, but he sure was puzzled.

Had that greedy bastard simply

wanted to avoid the balance of his high fee? Somehow that didn't ring true.

One thing was for sure. Or should that be two? One, he would eventually find out the reason. Two, he would pay out Whitman before that double-crossing son of a bitch got the chance to try again!

He took a swig of coffee. It was just the way he liked it, black and extra strong. And gazing northwards over the treetops and feeling the strength surging through him, he realized what it was he needed most now. The restoring, restful thing he always sought after Old Man Death had breathed too close.

Solitude.

★　★　★

'So, what happened that night, Mr Shiloh?' The girl still insisted on calling him that even though he'd corrected her several times. She was simply keeping him at arm's length, he supposed. If she figured she could dominate him that way she was badly mistaken. He felt he'd been armoured against every hurt known all his life. Bullets might hurt him, but likely that was about all.

Without reservation he furnished a full account of the gun contract he'd taken out on Ford Gabriel. She sat in silence, hearing him out.

Then, after a thoughtful silence, the inevitable query: 'But why, after you had gotten rid of Gabriel to open the way for Whitman to return here for his political campaign — why would he suddenly want to try to kill you?'

He shrugged.

'I guess high-rollers like him don't always need reasons. They are big players and they move places and people around like poker chips. But I've got no clear-cut answers. I was working for him, I did a job — you know about that — and when he and his gunners showed up in Sweet Creek they were coming after me and I don't have any notion why. Lucky for me they weren't up to the job.'

He rarely discussed how he made his living. This was different. Whitman had turned Judas on him, so he now owed the man nothing. Well, nothing but six in the guts if he got the chance.

There were more questions and he answered them all.

Father and daughter studied him in silence. He sensed they might well be thinking: *Who would contract to kill a man simply for money?* They did not understand his world. While ever there were raw and remote regions such as this waiting for civilization to catch up — until they finally had law and order with judges perched on high benches and sheriffs on every Western street — it would be the law of the strong. And the strong would always need men like him.

This sounded simple to him but maybe not to everybody.

'Well, you must have some notion why Whitman tried to kill you at Sweet Creek,' Jill pressed. 'Do you think the man is crazy!'

'Not him. He had some reason to want me dead . . . and for everyone to know he killed me. I might find out what it was before I give him six slugs up close against that fancy waistcoat of his.'

At another time and place such a statement might have deeply shocked. But the gun had long dominated the War God Hills. With no law, men settled grievances and challenges any way they might, usually with guns. The town had lived under the gun rule of Ford Gabriel a long time, and had reason to fear that Whitman might intend returning here for political reasons, now his way had been cleared by Gabriel's violent demise. Doubtless if he did, he would do his electioneering with lavish spending backed by six-gun security.

'You almost sound as though you admire him for such savagery,' the girl said mildly.

'That's too big a word, Jilly. But I respect him. Anybody who plays the game as hard as he does has got to be respected.'

'Well,' said Ben Flynn, 'we folks here certainly don't respect him, less so than ever after what happened in Sweet Creek.' The blackmith raised big hands and dropped them to his thighs again. 'Well, I suppose with Ford Gabriel dead and gone, the whole thing will start all over again.'

'The whole thing?' Clint queried. 'What do you mean?'

'Dad is saying we expect Whitman to seize control and take up where he left off before when he was driven out of the high country by someone stronger,' Jilly explained. 'You realize, of course, that man once boasted a strong political base here in the War God Hills, don't you?'

Clint nodded and she continued.

'Before we stood our ground after Shakespeare Jones hired Gabriel to protect us, Whitman made life here almost impossible with his arrogance and greed. We simply expect it to be the

119

same all over again now. Dad believes Whitman will take up just where he left off. That he'll be king of the high country again . . . and all the votes that go with such control.'

The gunfighter began pacing about restlessly. His feet were itching. Yet there were still answers he was curious to seek.

'Tell me about Gabriel,' he said. 'What kept a top gun like him protecting the War Gods against Whitman for next to nothing?'

Jilly shrugged.

'You might not understand. I'm not certain we do, really. But, as I see it, Gabriel was a lonely man when he showed here, and when he realized we needed protection from Whitman he perhaps saw a way to connect with real people — a chance to stop being alone. So he approached Shakespeare who realized his worth, then flattered and soft-soaped the gunman until he agreed to protect us for next to nothing.'

'He was almost impossible to like,'

her father remarked. His lips quirked. 'Much like Shakespeare is himself, I guess. Still, he scared most folks, and was lethal with that pistol of his until — '

The man broke off, studying Shiloh quizzically. The gunfighter shrugged. Folks just didn't understand him or his life. Had he not taken up the Colt and mastered it he would have been dead at fifteen. He would never apologize for how life had shaped him.

'He sounds like a born loser to me,' he said roughly. 'In the end I reckon he either just got slow or soft . . . which is the same as getting dead in our business.'

The blacksmith grunted and went out, leaving the girl to fuss about settling her patient down for the night. He didn't respond to her soft, 'Good night,' as she disappeared, leaving him with his thoughts.

And with his old enemy, loneliness . . .

There was no man he feared. But

what about the lonesomeness, gun-fighter? All those nights with only ghosts for company . . . the same ghosts that had haunted Gabriel, maybe? What about all the women who would never share a gunman's life, and the men who always feared and distrusted you?

He reined in his thoughts, just in time. That was mawkish stuff — he only lapsed like that when either hurt or lonesome. He lighted a cigar and soon self-assurance returned.

He would ride in the morning, he knew now. And wondered why the parable of Gabriel had moved him so little. He believed Gabriel had slowed, which was why he was in the ground. By contrast, he was faster than he'd ever been, had proven so in Sweet Creek. He was Clint Shiloh, as armoured against lonesomeness as he was against the guns of his enemies. Or most of them, leastways, he corrected ruefully, fingering the spot where a staggering drunk's wild bullet had come so close to killing him.

He lighted a cigar and studied the cards fate had dealt. There was a joker in the deck now, he knew. For whether he liked it or not, he was now deeply in their debt up here. The Clint Shiloh who would never succumb to loneliness or weakness was the same man who never left any debt unpaid, whether it be honourable or otherwise.

He owed these folks plenty.

He would repay them and maybe even find a way to help them. But before that, there was something he must first do, something he always did after Old Man Death breathed too close. And thinking of this he was almost at peace within himself as he lay listening to the night wind blowing restlessly across the rooftops of Durant.

★   ★   ★

A tarnished yellow sun was smoking in the west the day Marcus Whitman set out on the final leg of his long-awaited return to Durant and the War God Hills.

Dapper, ramrod erect and full of himself, just as the high country remembered him last, the Assembly candidate wore a smile fixed to his face as his cavalcade topped out the last rise and approached two ranchers drawn up on the side of the trail in their buckboards a mile south of the town which was his destination.

He was smiling because he was again playing out the role of the Whitman of the past, the benevolent landlord, politico and visionary who had at last returned. What matter if the yokels suspected he'd recently hired a gunfighter to rid himself of Gabriel? He had the words, the money and the know-how to mould people and manipulate them, even while conceding this task could prove high risk in the early stages.

Some of these country hicks had long memories. Yet if words, personality, confidence and fat political promises could change things round, then he was the man for the job.

In retrospect, he was amazed by the

way he'd shilly-shallied so long simply from fear of just one lousy gunman. But he quickly thrust that aside as he reined in to greet the locals with a wave and a big smile.

'Good to be back, gentlemen.' He searched for names. 'Er, Mr Wallace and Mr Pitt, isn't it? Looking forward to seeing you at our first meeting. I'm calling it 'Whitman For Denver!' Sure hope you enjoy it.'

The ranchers appeared unimpressed. Eventually one man scowled while the other deliberately spat over his wagon wheel.

Whitman was frowning as they moved on. Yet only momentarily. He must be patient, he counselled himself. For when the towners and ranchers of War God Hills had rebelled and virtually kicked him out of the county before, even Whitman himself acknowledged he'd treated them badly up here.

Well, he was back, thanks to Shiloh. And even though already mentally totting up all the grudges and unpaid dues he held against these 'hill-billies', retribution would wait. He had ground to recover and fences to mend here if he wanted the population to accept his return and eventually use their voting rights to boost him into the State House in Denver come election day.

It would only be afterwards, when back in full control, that he might get to consult his 'get square' list and set about evening some old scores.

The party topped out the final rise and the town lay directly ahead.

Whitman rode up front with Emil Durkin on his right. Big Durkin had taken a flesh wound in the leg during the shootout at the Devilrider and still walked with a slight limp. The hardcase kept his right hand close to gunbutt. He was not as confident of a warm welcome back to Durant as Whitman appeared to be.

In back of the two lead riders came Whitman's 'insurance,' three flinty gunmen replacing his Sweet Creek losses. The trio had demanded and got a big increase in money, following the violence already encountered. 'Risk money,' they'd termed it, and Whitman had no option but to pay up.

He begrudged paying any man one cent more than he must. But this was no time for thrift. For the shoot-up at the Creek had sent shock waves rolling up into the hills which must now be counteracted.

He felt satisfied with the gun power he'd mustered, although he begrudged paying Woodstock and Curran $100 a week apiece. To offset that, he regarded the third man, Bob French, cheap at $150. Tall and impressive, French was a lethal rising talent, exactly the sort of man you needed at a time like this.

He summarized the situation optimistically: Shiloh shot up and most likely dead; the region in fear of him all over again, and with reason; Gabriel in his grave where the bastard belonged; and the damaging Sweet Creek shoot-up hopefully already fading into the background.

Not great, but not bad either.

He touched a vesta to a cheroot and inhaled luxuriously. Maybe if things continued to go his way now he might soon be in a position to fire Woodstock and Curran and simply retain Durkin and the lethal French. Two top guns to keep a bunch of red-nosed country hicks toeing the line sounded workable right now.

Already he was rehearsing his pitch in his thoughts. With every independent section-owner in the War God Hills qualified to vote he must brush up on his techniques and identify their needs and concerns. He should also hone up on the best ways to convince them just how much better off the region would become with himself elevated to the legislature and personally thrusting their needs forward before the most powerful body in Colorado.

His thoughts were interrupted when Durkin drew abreast as they rode past the first buildings. 'We're expected by the looks, boss man,' he muttered.

Only now did Whitman grow aware of the small crowd assembled ahead in the main street before the Busted Luck Saloon, and even at a distance you could sense the hostile mood.

'You sure this is gonna be as friendly as you figured?' Woodstock growled when Whitman's raised hand brought the party to a halt. 'Don't look all that hospitable to me.'

Eyes narrowed, Whitman sat considering. These rubes must have heard by now how he'd gone after Shiloh. That gunner had made a lot of friends here the day he put Gabriel in the ground, with only a minority of citizens who'd profited under that gunman's protection not welcoming the final outcome. Yet if Shiloh was dead, as appeared pretty certain, then these hicks would be dumber than even he thought should they intend trying to rid themselves of him a second time.

Yet maybe that was the case.

'Want me to go on ahead and get the lay of the land afore you come on in, boss man?' French offered.

Drawing assurance from the gunmen's support, Whitman shook his head.

'No, that'd only give them confidence. We go in as planned. We come peaceable and I'll do all the talking. If things get out of hand I'll signal, but I believe I can handle this.'

The party swung around the dilapidated old barn and entered the central block. The wind fluttered the flag atop the Durant Hotel. The towners stood before the saloon and Whitman picked out the flamboyant figure of the mayor up on the saloon porch, sunlight glinting on silver hair. There was a scattering of men in working flannels and levis, several women in poke bonnets.

None appeared friendly.

But Whitman's smile was broad and seemingly genuine.

'Ah, my old friends!' he beamed, and tipped his hat to the Joneses on the porch. 'What? Not going to welcome my overdue return, Mayor?'

'Avaunt!'

'Pardon?'

Shakepeare Jones struck a pose, ready to deliver a damning denunciation. But the words died on his lips as he noticed young French drop a hand on to Colt butt, an action which immediately caused the windy mayor to go stepping backwards and fumbling for the smelling salts.

Whitman grinned. Nothing had really changed, he realized. They'd let him walk all over them before they finally rose up and kicked him out; there were suddenly signs they might be ready to crumble again.

But before this could happen, opposition in the squat shape of Joe Crook appeared. Runty and irascible, Crook had grown strong under Gabriel's protection and that strength had not vanished for Crook with the gunman's death, as it had done for most.

'Well?' Whitman challenged when Crook swaggered forward. He noted the man's new air of toughness. 'Where is my welcome home? What's the matter with you people?'

Crook cleared his throat.

'I reckon you ought to be able to figger that better than just about anybody, Whitman.'

'Well, you'll have to forgive me but I've no notion what you're griping about — '

'Was it you that had Gabriel killed?'

It was a man in back who yelled the question. But immediately a redhead at his side rounded on him and shoved him violently.

'What if he did, Murphy? Gabriel was a son of a bitch and deserved all he got!' the man shouted. 'He only favoured fools like Shakespeare and a handful like him, but the rest of us were glad to see him in a casket.' He raised his voice. 'Ain't that right, folks?'

The spontaneous cheer that welled up saw Whitman lean back in his big Texas-Spanish saddle. At last he was smiling, sensing that Gabriel, while a hero to some, seemed not to have stood as high with the majority as he'd feared.

'I had nothing to do with Gabriel's death — ' he began, but broke off when Shakespeare began whipping them up again.

'Quiet them down!' Whitman yelled in sudden temper. The man who responded fastest was his young gun, French. He heeled his horse deliberately into the mob and knocked two men heavily to ground.

That started it.

The dust-up that ensued involved a score of combatants, was quick and brutal. But Whitman's professionals were up against amateurs, and it was only a matter of time before the newcomers were back in control again.

'All right!' Whitman shouted. 'I came here today to make my peace and offer you your rightful part in a better future. I still intend doing just that, but I won't permit violence to replace open debate and discussion. You leave me no choice. Boys, clear this street!'

It was the last thing the troublemakers had anticipated — naked six-guns threatening them on all sides. And when Shakespeare Jones grew overexcited and leapt atop a crate and began haranguing, French sprang forward and belted him unconscious with a vicious cut of six-gun barrel.

It was the sight of their flamboyant mayor sprawled motionless in the dust that brought the incident to a sudden halt.

And when young French leapt atop a water barrel and fired three evenly spaced shots into the sky, the quietness came down and all knew the feeble rebellion was over.

A blind man could tell Whitman was fully back in charge once again.

7

Man Alone

The afternoon sky was dotted with fleecy cloud puffs drifting in slow procession like leaves in a stream, floating west. Soon the sun was sinking towards the hills and only then did the man stir, rising to clamber up over the pile of grey rocks that brought the full sweep of the entire valley into view.

The cigarette clamped between the gunfighter's teeth was unlit. This was a mile above the War God Hills where fleeting shadows raced across the rocks and trees of the wind-blown hilltop to go rippling down the slopes before dropping away into canyons in a race that could never be lost or won.

It was working, Shiloh realized with satisfaction. It had never failed him, this instinctive retreat to solitude in the aftermath of gunsmoke or maybe a close brush with death.

He didn't know if other men of the gun sought solitude at times like this. He only knew what worked for him.

Or did it . . . ?

That query which jumped unbidden into his mind took him by surprise. What could it mean? He rarely entertained regrets, so what was the inner Shiloh trying to tell him?

That he'd had enough?

Impossible!

He shook his head and dismissed the thought. Men like him never quit. They kept going until . . .

He went no further than that. He never did. And yet, with increasing frequency these days, whenever he started in daydreaming it seemed the dream always turned serious and he was likely to hear an inner voice whisper: *Had enough, gunfighter? They'll get you sure if you don't quit . . .*

He realized the sun was gone. Out across the mighty canyons, broken ridges and gnarled cliffs still held the sun's fire, but here on the pinewood crest all was shadowed and still.

Soon it was totally quiet.

He gathered up an armload of fuel and quickly had the fire going.

The horse watched him from a distance and the wind feathered its mane. The buckskin was no longer young, but still strong. In the animal's eyes the man seemed to sense nostalgic memories of other camp-fires and far-off places shared on nights such as this.

As he ate, stars appeared point by point in the deepening sky and he could feel all uncertainty draining away from him until full strength and resolution had returned.

Yet again, death had nearly claimed him. But he'd prevailed. And having done so he knew he would finish repaying the people who'd almost certainly saved his life, then move on. Yet again.

A frown cut dark brows.

At other times like this when he went through this solitary ritual in order to recover and renew his strength, he quickly got to thinking clearly again until his future appeared direct and uncomplicated: get riding, take another job, move on. But this time the vision in his mind's eye of Clint Shiloh riding off on the high lonesome again looking for action as he'd done all his life seemed to lack the old pull and the excitement.

How come?

The night held no answer. But the feeling continued to niggle at the edges of his mind until suddenly the huge bloated moon came sailing up from out of the ravines. Instantly the black night sky turned the deepest of dark blues, and all the stars were bright.

And he realized that nagging feeling had left him and he was once again the uncomplicated man of the gun, calm and sure. He knew that by first light he would feel ready again for his world and the dangers . . . the only world he really knew.

But for now he must rest.

He took the ground sheet from his pack, drew the bright blue blanket over himself and only an uncaring moon knew where the gunman slept.

* * *

His forge was cold!

Ben Flynn stood staring at the dead grey ashes choking the grate in disbelief. He never allowed his forge to extinguish completely. not even on Sundays. So how in hell . . . ?

Then slowly comprehension hit. Of course! Last night had been the kind of evil night when a man might even forget his name or religion — a night of furtive midnight meetings in a harness shed and then later down in Wal Bruning's cellar. Whenever solid men he'd thought he'd known well grew over-excited and angry and talked about gathering what Bruning had called 'a citizen's army' to march on the hotel where the 'invaders' were housed

. . . surely a man could be excused for forgetting just about anything!

They'd taken no action, of course. Just griped and cussed and parted at last to go trudging off to their homes in the small hours to drop into bed exhausted . . . without a thought for fires or forges . . .

The blackmith was a weary man as he quit his foundry and trudged across the house yard. It was a bright morning in Durant, one of those bitter-sweet days when the chirping of birds and the lowing of Tommy Hudson's milch cow should have had a calm and reassuring effect. Yet instead everything seemed to jar somehow, as though the world was slightly out of kilter.

Which, of course, it was.

In the the final analysis he knew it was Durant's own fault. Firstly, they'd made the mistake of permitting a killer to protect them when Gabriel came to town. Then when that hardcase went down, almost overnight he was being replaced by the man they genuinely feared, Whitman. The ruthless politico had cleared the way for his return here with bullets and gunmen, and was already spreading his money, influence and in some cases, charm, throughout the town and surrounding countryside.

Even now, the blacksmith found it hard to believe everything had panned out so well for Marcus Whitman here, despite that bloody business down at Sweet Creek.

And the weakening thought made itself felt now: would it not be simpler and better just to give in? Let Whitman alone to pitch his political spin and even support him in his quest for a seat in the legislature. It could save a lot of pain and uncertainly, and maybe even lives, long term.

And who could be sure? Maybe Whitman might even be genuine this time. The man might settle for an honest campaign and accept the results, either good or bad.

Encouraged by this thought the big blacksmith was mounting the rear steps to the kitchen when something caught the corner of his eye.

He turned sharply, and there it was! A hundred yards distant across the town square, it hung brightly flapping from the hotel's upper front balcony railing.

A bright yellow banner with the bold letters in crimson reading:

ASSEMBLY

VOTE ONE

WHITMAN FOR CLEARWATER!

It came as a shock even though he should have been ready for it. But somehow the sheer size and brazenness of that dominating poster hit him like a reality shock. It said there would be elections and Whitman would be the most powerful and best-prepared candidate.

And they would wind up with a criminal — likely a murderer — representing all these fine people in the

State's great house of government!

Yet surely Whitman's intentions had always been only too transparent, the sober side of his mind reasoned? Hadn't the man made statements to the press concerning his ambitions over at Bell City, had certainly not denied them during his brief stopover down at Sweet Creek.

Even so, the reality of that poster still struck him as a reminder of all that was wrong here . . . and that he and others as weak as himself had stood back and allowed it to go this far . . .

Turning, he glimpsed people standing in the dust of the square staring up at the thing. A couple scratched their heads in confusion.

'Dad!'

His daughter's voice. He glanced up and saw her in the window of the spare room, the one the gunfighter had occupied.

He pulled himself together. 'OK, coming, honey! Coffee on yet?'

The coffee was on the table and

growing cold by the time he actually got to the kitchen after being delayed by his next-door neighbour demanding what he intended doing about Whitman. Plainly he also had pulled the wool over his own eyes and refused to believe it would come to this, when Blind Freddy could see that it must.

'Are we as weak and foolish to stand by and just watch this happen, Ben?' the man had demanded. 'What are you going to do?'

'Likely the same as you, Lawson!' he'd retorted gruffly. 'Nothing, is what!'

He'd dropped into his chair and taken a badly needed jolt of tepid coffee before he suddenly frowned and raised his head.

Was someone singing on a black day such as this? Didn't make sense!

His daughter entered the room, kissed the back of his head and crossed to the stove. She'd ceased singing but only to begin humming. Surely a man could only take so much?

'Do you mind — madam!' That was a tone and a term reserved for only when sorely vexed.

Jilly Flynn turned and smiled brightly. She looked as pretty as he'd ever seen her, which only seemed to irritate him the more.

'Right now I'm fixing your eggs, Dad. After that I will — '

'You know what I mean, damnit! You must have seen that damned poster — and you know about last night! How can you be cheerful on the worst day we've ever had?'

She sat down with a cup of coffee and spoke to him quietly and calmly. Of course she understood why he was upset and why the whole town seemed to be in shock. And yet she still did not seem concerned, or even particularly worried. Why not, she asked rhetorically? Because she had faith, he was told.

'Faith!' he sputtered. 'Look, just because you womenfolks traipse off to church at the drop of a — '

'Not that kind of faith,' she said, hopping up to begin tidying the bench. She paused and glanced over her shoulder. 'I'm talking about faith in Clint.'

His jaw sagged.

'Faith in Clint!' he repeated dully. 'Whitman rides in like Custer on parade with a bunch of guns and virtually takes over in a couple of hours. Then he tells us we're all have to vote for him — and on top of all that you want me to put my faith in a gunman who's already cut and run! I tell you that —'

'No, *I'm* telling *you* something for a change, Dad. Clint told me he would be back. I certainly don't want him to do that if it means danger for him. Yet I do have faith in him and I feel you should also.' She smiled. 'More eggs?'

The burly blacksmith made no reply. First the forge, then the banner, now his daughter talking like a fool. He could not be certain, but offhand this felt like the worst day of his life . . . and of the town's.

Only one thing to do, as he saw it.

He grabbed down his hat and headed for the saloon. He needed to get good and drunk!

8

On the Campaign Trail

'Honesty and integrity in government is the very least you fine frontier folk can expect from your elected representatives in the State House!' the speaker said with deep sincerity. 'And that is something that I, as your elected representative, will guarantee to every single one of you gathered here tonight.' A pause for effect, then, 'I hope you all believe me?'

The response was muted at best, the City Meeting Hall barely a quarter full.

Even so, some forty or fifty citizens, mostly women and maybe a dozen or so reluctant husbands still constituted a bigger turn-out than anyone in town might have expected earlier, when a worried Whitman was hiring people to march around banging drums and announcing the town's first formal political gathering in years — free food and drink provided!

It was likely the free vittles that attracted most. Yet those who'd turned up more out of curiosity than any other reason were soon feeling pleased they'd done so.

For Whitman was good. He'd always been a naturally gifted speaker and it was this talent more than any other that had earned him his nomination for the Democratic ticket back in mile-high Denver.

Outside on the square the curious and the cynical were gathered in clusters or paced to and fro before the lighted windows streaming with bunting. Whitman had acted with such decisiveness in plunging directly into his campaign that some of his most vociferous foes, such as Shakespeare Jones, were yet to recover much ground.

This was an exciting night for the War God Hills and so far curiously lacking the violence and uproar most folks expected.

For after all, although respected, and in some places rightly feared, Whitman was no hero to most here. A lot of voters still believed he had likely contracted the gunfighter Shiloh to get rid of Ford Gabriel and so pave the way for his return to the high country. That factor alone could have been sufficient to generate a wave of civic protest tonight, yet this had not been the case.

A couple of old greybeards lounging at the saloon bar conjectured that, had Clint Shiloh only been on hand tonight, things would likely be very different and much more exciting. Maybe.

But the gunfighter was no place to be seen, had in truth not even been sighted since the day before.

Nobody could figure why.

★   ★   ★

From the darkened balcony of the Flynn house on Maple, Shiloh could see the glow of lights in the sky from the City Meeting Hall. A shadowy bulk in a deep chair nearby, Ben Flynn lighted his pipe and coughed to break the silence.

The gunfighter had been quiet since unexpectedly showing up just on dusk. Jilly had been excited to see him, her father less so maybe, yet still pleased.

Shiloh had unexpectedy grown on the burly smith, despite his objections to the grim trade he followed. Big Ben Flynn was a man of peace at heart and naturally regarded gunfighters with contempt.

Yet what impressed the big man at the moment was that, despite having every cause to hate Whitman as a man who'd tried to kill him, Clint now appeared to be acting with considerable restraint, not a quality the smithy would normally associate with a gunslinger.

'All sounds peaceful enough,' Flynn remarked at last.

Still no reponse.

' . . . So, I wonder if in light of that

we're to wonder if that high-stepper might have changed his ways and maybe turned over a new leaf, huh?'

Finally, Shiloh stirred and turned towards him. 'Not him. Whitman won't change — can't.'

'Then what's keeping them entertained so peaceably over yonder?'

'He's selling them a bill of goods, is what. Promise the world, toss in a few baubles and tell plenty lies. That's his style. And after he gets elected they'll never see him back here from one year to another.'

Jilly appeared at that moment and her father heaved to his feet and excused himself. Claimed he needed an early night in order to be fresh just in case all the peacefulness and fine words across at the meeting hall should suddenly erupt into violence, he remarked with a grim smile as he left.

'Do you expect that to happen, Clint?' Jilly asked.

'Huh?'

He hadn't heard what either had

said. It was as though his mind was in another place, and this was just his lean frame leaning here against an upright with a lighted cigar between the fingers on this uneasily quiet night.

'What's wrong, Clint? You've been like this ever since you came back from . . . from wherever it was you went.'

When he turned and looked at her she realized she'd never seen him so serious, not even when he was laid up, with her nursing him.

He had good reason for this mood, which hadn't claimed him until he returned to Durant to discover that Whitman had already arrived. He'd not expected the big man to show up this fast or in such strength, although he realized belatedly that he maybe should have done.

There had been but one brawl earlier, yet it was over quickly with little damage done. Then within the hour the Whitman party had arrived in force on Main to set up shop at the City Meeting Hall, and a neighbour had reported a reasonable crowd up there with no sign of trouble, as yet.

All this had been unexpected. But what was even more so, for Shiloh, was his own reaction.

For the brutal fact was that the man doing all the talking over there on the square was the same man who had contracted him to kill Ford Gabriel, welched on the balance of his fee, then had come close to putting him in his grave down at the Creek. The man whom he knew without doubt could only bring disaster on this town in the long run if not reined in.

How much more reason did a man need to stand up and strike back?

That was his firm intention on riding in from the mesa country following his ritual night alone, wrestling with his dreams, regrets and something new — an almost overwhelming sense of obligation and responsibility.

In that hour, the stage had seemed set for a showdown.

Maybe it still was — but Shiloh

would not be playing any role in it. Not now he'd taken time to think it all through and make fresh plans, he wouldn't.

That hour alone in a back street bar nursing an untasted whiskey, was maybe the most significant in his life.

For his soul-searching had forced him to acknowledge that any intervention he might make must inevitably lead to gunplay, for Whitman would brook no hindrance at this late stage, would allow nobody to challenge him again.

And yet, what option did this gunfighter have but to play his hand out as he knew he should? He was the man of the gun . . . so should be ready to make his stand on behalf of this town and be ready to back it with bullets if he must.

What was holding him back?

And the answer had come, bullet fast and brutal.

He didn't want to gunfight anyone . . . not even the man who must be taken down.

He turned his head towards the house, haggard lines of uncertainty furrowing lean cheeks as he saw Jilly and her father heading off for Main Street.

Would they understand why he must stand back . . . why he might have to leave? Not all of it maybe, for it would mean their saying goodbye. Now he could only draw on his cigarette and hope that in time she might get to understand how maybe a decision to ride out had been all for the best.

Maybe . . .

★ ★ ★

Shakespeare Jones was puzzled why the boardwalk audience he was addressing on the topic of 'political invaders' in their town was suddenly no longer paying attention. This was annoying enough to cause the mayor to forget his place. 'A cue!' he snapped at storekeeper Joe Crook. 'Where in the sacred name of eloquence was I, Joe?'

Crook didn't reply. The little man was staring fixedly past Jones, eyes wide behind his spectacles as a tall figure flanked by two gunmen and trailed by two riders came swinging around the street corner.

Whitman was smiling broadly as he came up; Jones turned pale.

'Evening, gentlemen,' Whitman greeted, 'I trust I'm not interrupting anything here?'

Jones swallowed, yet found the nerve to speak up.

'Begone, varlets!' He snapped. Then, thinking better of it, changed his tune, forced a smile. 'Ahh . . . we were just discussing something important, Whit — er, I mean, Mr Whitman.'

'Glad to hear it. Might I know what it was?'

Whitman appeared both genial and friendly. Yet the faces of Durkin and Harris at his side were like stone. Even so, after clearing his throat, Jones rustled up the the nerve to talk straight.

'We were actually speculating on the

oft-asked question as to whether it was you who had Ford Gabriel taken down — if you would know the truth, er, sir.'

Whitman frowned, was considering his response when a voice sounded somewhere behind.

'Of course he did!'

'Who dares say so?' Whitman snapped, turning sharply.

'It really doesn't matter who says it, Mr Whitman,' said Jilly Flynn, standing at her father's side. 'All that really concerns folks here is that we all know it to be the truth.'

Whitman's eyes appeared to change colour. He felt his campaign had got off to a flying start, all things considered. He'd been much reassured by the response of relatively placid audiences at his rallies thus far. But suddenly this night now seemed to take on a sharper edge.

'That's an evil assertion to make, young lady!' he retorted. 'You dare allege that I had Gabriel killed? Me . . . your soon-to-be representative at the Capital? Outrageous!'

'Folks are saying you had good reason,' Jones weighed in courageously, even if shaking in his boots. The blowhard mayor chose to overlook the fact he'd recently been overtly friendly with Gabriel, simply because the gunman scared him too much to be otherwise. Then, to his own astonishment, he found the courage to declare, 'Matter of fact, they're also claiming it was you and your bunch who tried to gun down Clint Shiloh at Sweet Creek, if it comes right down to cases.'

This drew a mutter of agreement from the onlookers gathering in the background along the plankwalk. Somehow this bright evening suddenly seemed to lend itself to speaking out, getting things off the chest.

Whitman plainly didn't like what he was hearing, but it wasn't finished with yet.

'You claimed in your letter to the mayor here afore you come back you was bringing only goodwill with you!'

159

charged the storekeeper on the fringes, drawing courage from numbers. 'You claimed you'd changed, but mebbe you ain't changed at all!'

'Enough, damn you!' Whitman was pale. 'I don't have to listen to this — '

'Indeed you do, sir!' Mercurial Shakespeare Jones was suddenly fired up and determined to have his say. 'We feel you've done us a great disservice here, Mr Whitman. We were so afraid of you before we were even obliged to find us a champion to defend us, and Brother Ford did a sterling job. Yet the moment he was gone you came swaggering back with your lies and promises and big talk — '

He got no further as a Whitman nod sent a signal to the mounted French in the background.

French was expert at certain things. He heeled his mount forward with a touch of steel. A woman screamed a warning to the mayor, but too late. French's six-gun swung in an are and Jones was knocked headlong when the

160

barrel thudded against the back of his silver-haired skull with a sickening thud.

His face suffused with fury, Ben Flynn lunged forward, then froze as the weapon in French's fist swung to cover him.

In the sudden ugly silence, Whitman stood tall and arrogant before them.

'If this is how you want it then this is how it shall be. I came here prepared to bury the hatchet and forget old differences. But you are forcing me to play a strong hand and I shall play it to the hilt. Now cart that bum off and clear this street. That's an order. Move!'

Whitman was conscious of an exhilarating feeling of power as he walked away trailed by his henchmen, not one voice lifted in protest now.

Of course, he'd regretted the time which he'd wasted while the deadly Gabriel had kept him away from this, the stepping stone to his ambitions. But now he was swiftly making up for lost time. Many of these people were either indebted to him, afraid of him, or both. He could bluff them and exert control, and would quickly weed out the toughest among them and get rid of them fast. Should any man refuse to knuckle under and help him gain what he should and would have, he could now have him 'disappeared', a technique he'd employed successfully more than once back in mile-high Denver during his climb to the top.

'No, not quite the top,' he reminded himself under his breath. '*The real top will only really be yours when you are seated in the State House . . . so this game is still afoot . . . Senator!*'

He had lapsed into this way of encouraging himself more and more frequently since his return to the War Gods. But it was working for him. Each time he thought this way his strength and self-assurance lifted and he grew more and more confident.

He swaggered as he walked and none dared impede him as he made his way along the main stem flanked by henchmen, waving mockingly as curious heads appeared in windows and doorways.

Suddenly he slowed. He wasn't sure why, but he'd sensed something intrude upon his peripheral vision . . . something half-seen yet which seemed somehow to alarm . . .

He jerked around and felt ice run down his spine. Directly across the street on the saloon porch stood a tall, dark-garbed figure with folded arms staring directly across at him with eyes like chips of flint.

Whitman's mouth went dry as dust.

'Shiloh!'

The word reverberated in the sudden quiet and Jilly Flynn whirled to rush across the street. Still with folded arms, Shiloh remained focused upon the party the other side of Main as she rushed up to him.

'Clint!' she cried, using his given name for the first time. 'You shouldn't be — '

'Should be, and am, pretty woman.'

He stepped down past her and muttered, 'Don't move from here, this is my play.'

'But — '

That was all he heard. He was already halfway across the street before French seemed to remember he still had his six-gun in his fist. With a wild curse the mounted man was sweeping the weapon around when Shiloh's right arm blurred to come up with a fully cocked Colt .45 with its black muzzle staring the hardcase squarely in the eye.

'Drop it, you son of a bitch!'

A breathless moment of uncertainty. Then fingers and thumb unclenched and French's gun thudded into the street. Instantly Shiloh holstered his Colt and nodded to Whitman, who had turned pale.

'You looked scared,' Shiloh remarked, closing in. 'You don't like taking risks when you might be in the firing line, do you, Whitman? I noted that back in Sweet Creek.'

'I counted you dead,' Whitman said tonelessly. 'How — ?'

'I'd never die owing a debt, Whitman.'

Shiloh saw his words strike home. Whitman was scared. Shiloh didn't blame him. The man could not be sure whether Shiloh mightn't be crazy enough to cut loose and gun him down here and now, even if it meant he must almost certainly die under the guns of his henchmen. Shiloh enjoyed the man's uncertainty and let him sweat some before he spoke again.

'Well, seeing as we're finally face to face again, Whitman, maybe you'd like to tell me what Sweet Creek was all about?'

The tall man forced a smile. 'Look, Shiloh, it was all a mistake — '

'Forget it!' he cut him off. 'We'll settle that another time. The way I figure, you wanted to kill me to build yourself up in the eyes of these folk up here who believed you'd hired me to get rid of Gabriel. How right am I — you double-dealing bastard?'

Whitman was no fool. Times like this when he was no longer in full control he was always ready to play dumb, cowardly or crazy. Anything to make certain he survived to get square another day.

As he would.

He always did.

'Vamoose!' Shiloh snapped with a jerk of the thumb. 'Go on, all of you, get your sorry asses out of here. I won't say it twice!'

He was playing a high-risk game and knew it. But he also knew his enemy. He realized Whitman was raging behind that snappy jacket and four-in-hand tie. But, again, he felt confident in his bluff. And this proved out when, following a curt order from Whitman, the entire bunch trailed his tall figure striding away along the plankwalk . . . with half of Durant watching them go.

'Heck, that was mighty impressive, Mr Shiloh,' a councillor said nervously. 'But shouldn't you . . . or mebbe all of

166

us, have done something while we had them fellers off-balance?'

'I could not agree more,' piped up Shakespeare Jones, the blowhard who'd made not one squeak during the tense confrontation. The former actor inflated his chest and struck an heroic pose, but nobody was impressed. The mayor had been scared. They all were.

Yet all were seeing Shiloh in a different light now. Much of the ill will lingering after the shootout with Ford Gabriel seemed to have subsided, largely due to the friendship that had sprung up between the gunfighter and the respected Flynn family. Yet what impressed them most about Shiloh was simply his gunspeed and icy courage, qualities often in short supply upon the streets of their town.

The man in the street in Durant had no way of guessing how this unfolding grab for power and votes might play out. Rightly, Whitman scared them. Many were prepared to vote for him, simply out of fear. Some believed

Whitman might simply vanish back to Denver should he be voted into the legislature, but just as many wondered whether he might elect to stay on. Yet all of them, despite variant views and attitudes, were at that moment ready to side with Shiloh. With him and his Colt .45.

Yet there were doubters, plenty of them. There mightn't be a man unimpressed by the way the gunfighter had faced down a whole gang of gunpackers. Yet could you rely on any gun should, say, somebody wave enough dollars under his nose to persuade him to change horses midstream?

They could only wait and see how the game played out. But with Jilly Flynn it was different. She couldn't understand the reason Clint had just risked his life and didn't hesitate to demand an answer as the three headed back for the house on Maple.

He was slow in responding, still drained by the inner fight he'd had with himself before intervening on the street.

He still felt the same about the gun, yet had learned, to his relief, that his concern for these people walking at his side now was stronger than anything else.

How strong . . . he reflected, looking at the girl . . . he was more and more beginning to understand.

'Simple,' he said, deliberately off-handed. 'I don't like owing anybody, bright-eyes. You folks pulled me through when I was in bad shape. That put me in your debt. Maybe what happened just now squares the slate.'

She seemed unimpressed by this as they halted before the stables.

'Well, if it was simply a matter of owing, and nothing more, then you can feel satisfied — and free of your debts — right now. You have repaid us.'

'Not quite.'

'What do you mean, Clint?' asked Ben.

'Another thing I never do is leave a job before it's finished. I'm expecting Whitman to strike back. He's looking to take over and he'll never rest with me cluttering up the landscape.' He nodded. 'So, I'll just hang around until he makes his move. I'll play out that hand as it's dealt, and only then we'll really be all square.'

Jilly was pale.

'And that's the only reason you'll be staying on?' she said accusingly. 'To square imagined accounts?'

'Well — ' he began, but already the girl had whirled and hurried off down-slope for the house. He called after her but she didn't look back. Shiloh shrugged. She had no call to get upset by the truth. Or did she?

But if what he'd just said was the truth, he asked himself, why was he now wishing he'd kept shut?

Without a word to a bemused Flynn, he spun on his heel and strode off. The hell with it! Just so soon as he'd seen Whitman either win his crummy election, or get kicked out by himself or somebody else, he would be on his way. What did it matter if they looked upon

Clint Shiloh as the man he believed himself to be, or as just another Ford Gabriel, looking only for glory or the dollar?

Did he give a rap one way or another?

He darted a glance back at the lights of the house and turned up the collar of his jacket as the night wind bit, then set out to prowl the town's outer perimeters until moonrise.

*　*　*

The craggy peaks of the Celinda Mountains glowed dull red in the setting sun and it was as if the War God Hills were dominated by the rim of a vast volcano. The first stars showed faintly in the darkening sky as the sun vanished with a rush, and from lower down came the howling of coyotes welcoming the night.

Leaning back in a plush velvet chair in the diner of the hotel, Marcus Whitman drew deeply on a cigar, totally ignoring the splendid meal spread before him. Cutlery gleamed and serving girls hovered, but he dismissed them with a curt gesture and dragged smoke deep into his lungs.

'Perception!' he growled aloud, and the drink waiter in the background stared uncertainly, not sure if he was being summoned or not.

But Whitman was in that moment unaware of everything but the irony and bad timing of the afternoon behind him.

On the surface it didn't seem much, he realized. Just a brush with Shiloh. No real fireworks. Not any blood spilled. And yet surely he could feel the ground shifting beneath his feet.

How come?

So simple. Out of nowhere he'd met up with Shiloh again just as he was gaining ascendency over this crummy town along with its lousy yet all important voters!

Perception was everything, as he liked to say. He'd been force-feeding the hicks on the perception that he was the candidate with the firepower and ruthlessness to make life hell for them if they failed to support his candidacy. Or someone who could just as easily turn the War Gods into their Promised Land should they simply all come together and vote him into the State House in Denver.

He had been riding high and growing stronger every day with his meetings and speeches — in his mind he had long since counted Shiloh dead, or at least gone — when out of nowhere that hardnose was suddenly back.

Now that guntipper had walked all over him before the whole lousy town!

Sure, his henchmen kept trying to convince him that the clash on the street really meant nothing; that Shiloh had simply got the jump and caught them off-balance somehow. He knew better.

The way he saw the big picture he'd just succeeded in grabbing back valuable lost ground with the voters and had them beginning to accept him as the genuinely strong man they needed, when an enemy shows and treats him like the hired help!

It was really nothing — or so Emil Durkin kept reassuring him. That showed how little that big gunshark knew about politics and, yes, perception.

As recently as that morning he'd had the whole town touching the forelock whenever he went by. But tonight, the same bakers, liverymen, white-collar businessmen and hired help who'd witnessed his one-man confrontation and dismissal, strode right on by without so much as a nod of the head.

He was heading for rock bottom!

Yet before he found the will and energy to start in gearing himself up again, things began to happen.

The first was when brawny Durkin pushed his way into the dining-room against instructions then brazenly dropped into a chair opposite to fix his employer with a mean yellow eye.

'Look here, damnit — ' Whitman began. But his brawny lieutenant had come to speak, not listen.

'Boss man,' he growled emphatically, 'you must know what's gonna happen if things go on like they done today, don't you?'

Whitman looked dull-eyed, almost a stranger. 'You tell me.'

'They're gonna win, is what. That Shiloh — '

'The hell with him! Get to the point.'

'He's gotta go, boss. He's gotta go and right now. Tonight! Otherwise — Hey, what you doing, boss?'

What Whitman was doing was suddenly getting to his feet, standing, and there was a glitter in his eye the other had not seen since that night down in Sweet Creek. Yesterday, Whitman had suddenly felt as if he'd been drugged, his strength sapped by one humiliating reversal, today it had only taken his henchman to march in on him and talk to him as if he was some loser, and all the Whitman vanity, ambition and natural-born ruthlessness were back. And it felt better, almost, than winning an election must feel.

'You are right, damnit. I guess I just needed someone to have the guts to remind me what I should have done the day we rode in.'

The rugged Durkin's eyes stretched wide. 'You mean — ?'

'Of course I do.' Whitman was striding from the room like a man inspired. 'Get the bunch together! Pronto!'

The gunman's eyes were blurring from whiskey and excitement.

'Good as got, boss man!'

9

Gunsmoke on Main Street

More than ever it was his custom at such times to seek the solitude of the wilds. Not saloons and gambling halls or travelling by train to some new quarter of the far-flung West. Rather, to head for the great vastnesses of mountains, valleys and streams until you finally knew you were ready to come back down to shave, don a clean shirt and make for the nearest town. Whichever town he chose there was always work on offer once they heard his name and had a chance to size him up. There was always work for a class gun — always.

Camped high in the Spur Creek Ranges he'd hunted above the timber-line, fished for trout in crystal mountain brooks, sat long into the nights cross-legged like an Indian in front of his fire.

That night a grizzly came into his camp, drawn by the scent of food. Man and beast studied each other across dancing flames, the great beast emitting murderous rumblings from deep in its hairy belly, the man silent, unblinking and unmoving.

After a long spell the bear appeared to grow uncomfortable under that stare, and with a final grunt of defiance, dropped to all fours and went shambling off into the blackness.

The gunfighter frowned pensively as sounds of the animal's retreat faded. What had scared the big critter off? Was it its failure to scent fear in him? Or might it be that it took one killer to know another?

He dismissed that thought on what proved to be his last night in the Choctaw Skylands. When a man began to tire of his own company — or started in brooding on what he was or might not be — it was time for a change.

He'd hoped this taste of solitude would clear his head and point out exactly what he must do, how he should be thinking. It had gone some way towards that, but there were still unanswered questions. Like, had he quit with the gun? Or, why couldn't he get her out of his mind? And, surprisingly, the most persistent — why couldn't he quit fretting about that lousy town?

Maybe what he really needed now was bright lights, rye whiskey and wild women — all of which he'd eschewed in preference to coming to hell and gone up here?

He packed up and headed for Jawbone.

There could well be news from the War God Hills to be had at the crummy little outpost on Wolf Creek.

During time he'd spent in Jawbone earlier, the locals had gone out of their way to be friendly. All knew his profession, but as he was the first top gunslinger to stop off at their rough little cowtown, they'd been none too sure how different he might prove to be from 'normal' men.

Now they watched him covertly as he strolled ino the saloon then toted his whiskey bottle to a back table.

Shiloh splashed spirits into his glass, downed a double shot, then poured another and leaned back leisurely. The looks and whispers left him unfazed. This sort of thing happened all the time in his line of work.

But Tough Kitty was not afraid. The only percentage girl in the place, she considered this stranger with the tied-down gun strikingly handsome. Earlier she had approached, but his reaction to her flattery was to give Kitty five bucks to buy a new hat for herself and get lost.

But when she returned and his bottle had been lowered several inches, he stared up at her pokerfaced for almost a minute, then wordlessly reached out with his boot and pushed a chair clear of the table for her.

Kitty could not have been happier had somebody invited her to the Governor's Ball. She sat smiling and chatting and helping him drink his whiskey, scarce seeming to notice it was just a one-way conversation, with Shiloh offering little more than the odd, 'Yes,' or 'No,' or 'Have another'.

Even so, she persisted in trying to get him interested in her as the night grew older and the professor banged away at the old open-topped piano near the batwings, but it didn't prove easy.

For when he studied her, he saw her muddy brown eyes appear to turn a vivid shade of sparkling green, while her voice became that of a lovely young woman who'd never hustled a drink in any down-at-heel saloon and never would. And once he even called her 'Jilly' but she didn't appear to notice.

To top it all, he wasn't having much success at getting drunk either.

Around eleven the girl was called away to help in the kitchen in back. Relieved, he lit up, picked up a newspaper from the bar, blinked at a short paragraph in the bottom right-hand corner under the heading;

DEAD MAN IDENTIFIED

'Anything wrong, Mister Shiloh?' asked the barkeep as his hands tightened on the paper.

Clint didn't hear. He stared at the newspaper in an odd way. Next thing he screwed it up and flung it aside, and knocked his glass over as he strode out.

'Hey, where's good-looking?' Kitty wailed when she reappeared later with a plate of sandwiches.

'Gone,' grunted the barkeep. 'Read something in that paper, turned kinda tight-jawed then hightailed. Left half a pint of whiskey behind.'

Kitty snatched up the discarded paper and the man tapped the bottom corner.

'Something down there, I reckon . . . '

Kitty, no great shakes as a scholar, squinted and began to read aloud;

Body identified. The body of a man found outside Sweet Creek was identified as Joseph Crook, storekeeper of Durant. As yet nobody seems to know how this man came to be shot, or who killed him.

Kitty lowered the paper slowly. 'Don't get it,' she muttered. 'Why would something like some crummy little storekeeper going to Heaven set my good-looking feller storming off thataway?'

'Who knows, Kitty?' the barfly mused. 'But I guess what you gotta remember is that the gunfighter breed is mighty different from plain folks. Hey, what's this, Kitty? That ain't a tear I see in your eye, is it?'

'You gotta be drunk,' she retorted in her toughest style. Then, picking up the bottle by the neck, she made her unsteady way across the room to console herself with a hairy buffalo hunter who also had the crazy notion that she had tears in her eyes.

Whitman stared blankly at his lieutenant. 'He's back . . . and he's what, you say?'

'Waiting to see you,' panted pock-scarred Jack Curran. The blocky gunpacker jerked a thumb over his shoulder. 'He's down at the High Shot Saloon, boss. Looking meaner than a cut snake, so he is. You'd reckon somebody shot his mother — but all he's griping about is that fool Crook, who was begging for it anyways . . . '

The man's voice trailed away. Marcus Whitman stared at him for a long moment longer, then turned back to the card table. All were seated there tonight, the pack of hardcases who were never out of sight as the high-voltage campaign picked up greater momentum every day. He'd had three days of uninterrupted campaigning which had been only slightly affected by a drunken incident where one of his men had shot a dumb storekeeper in an argument over a bottle of rum.

But now this!

He'd figured they'd seen the last of Shiloh when he disappeared — again. Most everybody had thought the same, with the exception of the Flynns and a handful of other non-Whitman admirers. In light of Shiloh's disappearance. Whitman had actually cancelled the contract he'd offered to a top gunman he'd had travelling west from Denver to join him up here.

Now he was back!

From out of no place that hardhead had returned, drifting in on the wind and then making threats! All that seemed to make sense was that this gunner must be drunk, loco or both.

'So . . . what do you say, boss?'

He blinked, realizing it was Durkin who'd spoken. The burly gunfighter looked different, he thought. Several Shiloh-free days with the campaign going so well and with the election campaign results seeming more and more to favour Whitman over his Republican rival, now installed at the hotel, had seen Durkin acquire — and indeed the rest of the bunch to acquire — an enhanced sense of authority, sureness and self-confidence.

Whitman actually detected a glitter of the flinty eagerness in the gunman's eye now . . .

He felt himself reacting cautiously for a moment, stepping back from what this news and his hardcase's glance were suggesting. Go in hard now before that gunner even had time to think of raising any more hell. Take him down!

But when he turned and studied the others one by one, he realized it was not simply Durkin: Curran, Woodstock and Harris all wore the same expression. A period of unchallenged authority had moulded a bunch of gunfighters into the disciplined unit he'd really needed right from the outset of his Durant, War God Hills, campaign.

And, he reflected thoughtfully, maybe he would not have even noticed this strengthening of his gun crew, but for Shiloh's return.

Of course he realized the gunman's apparent challenge could prove to be nothing more than bluff and swagger. But could he take that chance of being wrong . . . ?

He shook his head sharply. No! This was a moment of truth. With no law up here other than that which his gunmen carried on their hip, it was the rule of the strong and he had the strength. There was a challenge and he could either deal with it or run the risk of losing everything.

For just a moment he conjured up a vision of mile-high Denver and the glittering impressiveness of the seat of legislative power, the Colorado State Assembly. Ritual, glitter, honour and — who could tell where it might lead? Washington?

He shook his head to clear it.

Here and now — that was where the game was. And calmly and deliberately he brushed aside all else until but one reality remained. This man posed a threat, of sorts, but he possessed the strength to put him in his grave.

Could anything be simpler?

Even though his features showed a sudden strength and sense of exhilaration, Whitman was coldly calm within as he hefted a bottle and tipped it to his lips. Then he drew the back of his hand across his mouth, and spoke with a powerful calm and certainty.

'Gentlemen . . . time to finish what we started at Sweet Creek!'

*   *   *

Shiloh stood in the shadows of the alley alongside the saloon as the slow thudding of hoofbeats sounded from the south side of town.

The dark shapes of riders appeared at the far end of the street, while beyond the wall at his shoulder Shiloh heard the saloon going quiet.

For the drinkers, too, had heard — and knew what it meant.

He looked up as Whitman gave a hand signal that saw the riders fan out to travel four abreast ahead of him as they travelled along Main at a shuffling walktrot. As they came on, the gunfighter saw windows go dark on either side of the street, felt he could almost hear the whispering and shuffling as hidden eyes watched the horsemen going by, and knew this was different from anything seen here before.

After half a block, tall and youthful Bob French pushed a little forward of the others, lamplight glinting on the long-barrelled six-shooter in his hand.

As the cavalcade clattered by the Busted Luck Saloon, Marcus Whitman raised himself in the stirrups and shouted;

'Shiloh!'

Shiloh's shoulders rolled smoothly inside his black shirt as he drifted deeper into the shadows. The whole block appeared to be growing rapidly darker now, as two of the gumen, on a signal from Whitman, swung down and, leaving reins trailing, cautiously approached the saloon to peer in over the batwings.

'Where is that son of a whore?' Curran shouted. 'He hiding behind the skirts in there?'

Frozen faces stared back in silence, and Curran seemed ready to enter when Durkin's deep voice sounded in back of him.

'You won't find him hiding in here. Hiding ain't his style — '

'Sure he's hiding,' broke in young French, dismounting. He raised his voice to a shout. 'Under a bed, that's where we'll find him! Hey, Shiloh, what are you scared of? I'll take you on alone if you want something to drag you out of your hidey-hole.'

No response. Gunmen stared at one another, tense and uncertain. All but Bob French, who came striding out into the centre of the street with his gun, yelling and taunting.

Somebody began to laugh but the sound cut off as sharply as if somebody had thrown a switch.

Shiloh's lean shape appeared silently from a doorway directly behind the horsemen and moved to the edge of the porch in full sight.

'Judas Priest!' Woodstock's voice was jittery as he shot a glance over his shoulder and almost dropped his .44.

Then, 'Why, hello at last, Shiloh!' Whitman called mockingly from a safe, full block distant. It was meant as a warning to alert them all, but there wasn't one of them unaware of him already, standing there on the shadowed porch in the half light.

'Still not too late to quit, Whitman!' Shiloh called. 'All you have to do is point out which one killed the store-keeper and the rest can vamoose!'

His self-assurance was chilling. Whitman began sweating and the already jittery Woodstock tightreined his mount backwards a little further.

He was the only one. The others stood fast, drawing strength from their numbers.

'The only pointing any of us will do for you, gunslinger,' French hissed, dropping into a crouch, 'is to point you in the direction of Boot Hill!'

His finger tightened on the trigger and Shiloh shot him between the eyes.

It was a brutal early loss for the pack, for young French had muscled his way up to their very top rank in recent weeks and they'd been relying upon him heavily tonight.

But before any gunman could begin to waver at the spectacle of French sprawled there in the street looking more like some poor kid than a gunfighter, they were jolted from their shock by Whitman's angry shouting, which saw them instantly rank up and get ready to strike back.

Only thing, Shiloh was gone.

He'd only required a couple of seconds to make the alley mouth. He ran swiftly the full length, burst into River Street, followed it for a block east, with the shooting and shouting on Main sounding muffled and somehow harmless, at a distance.

He cut into a gloomy side-alleyway that would take him back up into Main.

192

Woodstock whirled in his saddle fifty yards distant and his six-gun exploded as Shiloh dived full length for the printer's porch before his gun responded. The first bullet knocked Woodstock out of his saddle, his body slamming a porch upright with an ugly thud.

Shiloh spun like a dancer as Curran came charging him behind a bucking gun. But the man's fire was wild and Shiloh's single shot saw the rider knocked to the roadway, lurch erect and go staggering drunkenly across the saloon steps, leaking crimson.

The shadow of a gunman vanished towards the stables as Emil Durkin's gun began to yammer, blasting shot after shot at Shiloh's position.

Only thing, Shiloh was no longer there. At that moment he was halfway down the length of Crackerbarrel Lane and still gathering pace.

It was not a retreat. Shiloh knew exactly where his lead had gone, understood the mental effect his strikes would carry. One dead, two shot up, himself still unscathed. That amounted to a victory in the making, but only if he gave them time to realize they were out of their class. Then self-preservation should take care of the rest.

His strategy might have worked just fine but for Durkin.

Durkin was the old pro who'd had experience in showdowns like this. Still on horseback, the big man was moving fast as he followed a hunch and tracked out of Main to go pounding down by Jackson's. When he swung right it was to glimpse a dark figure running in back of the saloon.

His six-gun bellowed and Shiloh dived headlong, rolled twice and came up shooting from behind a packing crate.

Lead whipped by Durkin's face and smacked hard into timber as he rolled then touched off two shots in return.

Triggering fast with the drumroll of his gun thunderously loud, Shiloh kicked back beyond the corner, rippled to his feet and disappeared once again, punching fresh shells into his Colt as he ran.

Both Whitman and Harris tore after him recklessly. But he was gone from sight and their bullets found only fenceboards. Whitman hollered to his henchmen and they returned to the front street. Moments later, Shiloh's Colt spoke from another angle and someone else howled in pain.

Silence.

Shiloh gave it five minutes before he went looking. On Main, wounded men were bawling for a doctor. He climbed up on the hotel porch but drew no fire.

It was over.

* * *

It looked like a casualty clearing station in the war!

That was a grey-faced Whitman's reaction as he put his head round the doors at Doc Gleeson's a long hour later.

He didn't bother going in to check

on injuries or offer a sympathy he was far from feeling. They'd let him down, so they could suffer, survive or die and he wouldn't give a damn. He'd waited to show himself after the shoot-out until he'd heard Shiloh was drinking beer with the blacksmith at the saloon. Earlier, Whitman had saddled a horse and left it tied up at the Doc's hitch-rail, ready to head off for Sweet Creek.

No telling what might befall him should he hang around here now, nothing to be gained by lingering in the ashes of defeat.

Whitman was down, as he would readily concede when he quietly quit town by a back alley and pointed the horse's nose towards the lower valleys. What he would not concede by any stretch, was that he was out.

He couldn't quit. Too much of his time, money and dreams were tied up in that crummy town; he wasn't about to throw aside everything and all those accredited landowners, and voters, who still could, and would, make clear his path into the Assembly.

What he was already planning would cost him far more to pay for one man than it had done to hire his four top guns, all now either dead, wounded or too gunshy to be of any real value to him.

It was anything but the end of the line.

Viewed in retrospect now, it was certainly a stroke of pure luck that the high-priced gunman whom he'd first contracted, then fired when he no longer believed he needed him, had made it all the way to Sweet Creek before learning his services were no longer required.

Doubtless Kain would charge him double, just out of spite. Whitman was prepared to pay even more, if he must. His fight was not over yet. Maybe it was just about to begin.

★ ★ ★

She didn't criticize, made no complaints. It was as though she was so relieved to have him seated there before her at the house drinking whiskey and coffee while she attended his minor injuries, that she felt prepared to forego the opportunity to remonstrate. Or 'nag', as he might term it, though.

Shiloh was soaking up the peace and quiet.

It was always this way after the shooting stopped. Times like this, there was always a curious flat feeling that not even whiskey could lift. And each time, the recovery seemed slower and more painful, so much so that once or twice, recently, he'd actually considered quitting.

He wouldn't, of course. It was all he knew. Still, it was tough when a man spent his time dreaming of ploughing his own ground and trying to make scrawny beeves fatten up and start in breeding.

But he wasn't griping. No chance. He knew all the risks — risks which in this instance had paid off. But Old Man Death had been at his shoulder every moment and it was about as good as you could get to be able just to sit not moving a muscle, while your hearing slowly recovered from the brutal crash of gunfire.

And to look at her.

He couldn't deny it any longer, how he felt about the blacksmith's daughter. Before, he'd reckoned he was only attracted. But the long nights in the high country followed by tonight's joust with death had brought home the sweet reality.

He was in love for the first time ever, yet knew it would never lead any place.

Folks claimed gamblers and drunks made the worst kind of lovers, but he would back his roll on gunfighters in that contest by a country mile. A pretty woman had once told him to his face that men of his trade were 'the dregs'. He'd believed her then, did so still . . .

'Well?'

He blinked and looked up to see her standing before him.

'Huh?'

Jilly rested hands on hips. 'I asked if you were hungry?'

'Hungry?' He began to smile. Who but a woman would come up with a question like that while a man was still ready to drop to the floor at the first loud noise?

'What have you got?'

'Cheese and bread.'

'Then that's what I'll have.'

His smile faded as she disappeared into the kitchen. He glanced across at Ben but his thoughts were far away. They'd told him Whitman had disappeared. He breathed deeply. That character could run, but never far enough. Not from him, that was. But hunting him down and seeing him answer for what he'd unleashed here — that would have to wait. It was enough right now just to be alive and in this good house.

The way he was feeling, this gunfighter would be lucky to be still awake by the time the bread and cheese arrived.

10

This Was a Man

'Kain?'

Clint Shiloh's voice sounded rough-edged as he stared into the freckled face of rancher Tom Hatch. 'Cleveland Kain?'

'That's the party, Shiloh. Sounds like you know him, huh?'

Shiloh nodded his dark head. He knew of Kain. He'd never met the man but once had seen him in action.

Two years back . . . South Dakota badlands . . .

Three wolf hunters with a grudge rode into Silvertree in search of a man who'd slain one of their party in a gunfight. That man's name was Cleveland Kain and they had no trouble in finding him. For he was waiting for them on the street. From the hotel

201

gallery, Clint Shiloh had watched two men die and the third go down spilling blood in a mere handful of blazing moments.

Since that day, the notoriety of the man with the skull face and lightning guns had grown until today in many places he was referred to as the nonpareil.

Tom Hatch studied Shiloh curiously as they stood by the corrals of Hatch's Big H double-section spread in the late afternoon. The rancher, whose outfit was the easternmost of the War God Hills cattle spreads, had been feeding bran mash to an ailing mare when the gunfighter showed up astride his high-shouldered horse to enquire about events in Durant during his absence.

After a silence, the man said, 'What brings you back to the hills, Clint? We all figured when you left you'd gone for good.'

Clint Shiloh had almost believed it himself. Every gunfight these times was followed by longer and longer periods riding the High Lonesome, warring with himself and what he did for a living. But this solitary period had been cut short — how could he have foreseen that in quitting he would feel he was leaving part of himself behind? How could he have known that a girl with green eyes was going to haunt him, along with her folks, who had shown him the first true and unselfish kindness he'd known in his life?

Yet even while he'd been wrestling with his emotions and demons the time before this, it had merely taken the newspaper report on Joe Crook's death to see him mount Two Bits and head back for the high country.

On that journey from Jawbone he'd told himself he was returning to deal with Whitman because an innocent man had died as a fallout of his presence — a brawl with drunken gunmen. Yet, deep down, he'd sensed it was far more than that.

He'd found himself unable to shake loose of the truth that, after all the long years with just horse and gun, loner Ford Gabriel had stumbled upon something truly rare and unique — for him. Kindness and understanding — and despite the ongoing violence that was part of his way of life — the discovery of a kind of peace and promise up there.

And Shiloh knew it was those things he hungered for now. They said no gunfighter could ever find peace in his lifetime; that every man who lived by the gun would eventually die for it and because of it.

Yet he knew he was prepared to challenge that belief for a girl with green eyes and a town which had been kind . . .

But that decision had been made before his return, and before he heard again the name 'Cleveland Kain' and learned the man was already here, in Durant.

Kain!

The moment Shiloh heard that name he knew what it meant. And knew, in that same instant, that everything was instantly changed here. For Kain was king of the fast guns, and notoriously vicious by nature. Many experts claimed Kain was invincible, and amongst that number was Clint Shiloh himself.

'Shiloh — ?' Hatch broke in on his turbulent thoughts. 'You still ain't told me what brings you back to the hills.' The man's brow furrowed at a sudden thought. 'Hey, you ain't got any fool notion of going back to town, have you? I mean, Whitman hates your guts, and now with that new gunpacker of his ... ? Judas, man, you'd be a fool — '

'You must think I'm loco.' Shiloh's manner was tense as he swung his horse away. 'Why the hell would I want to go back there for any reason, much less now after what you've just told me. I only horned in on things down there in the first place to pay off a debt..and I paid that off in spades, if you recall.'

'Yeah, I sure do recall. Everyone does. Well, so long, Shiloh. Luck.'

'See you when the grapes get ripe, Hatch,' Shiloh called back. And pointed Two Bits west.

★   ★   ★

Ben Flynn blinked against the sudden light as he emerged from his back room into the parlour. The blacksmith stared at the clock on the mantel. Almost midnight. He frowned as he made his way through to the front porch.

'Jilly!' he called to the dim figure standing at the railing. 'What are you doing still up?'

The girl turned with the moonlight behind her. 'Oh, I'm sorry I disturbed you, Father. I . . . I just couldn't sleep.'

'Why not?' he demanded, joining her. 'Not worried about something, are you, honey? Not fretting about this latest dirty move of Whitman's?'

'No, really I'm not, Dad.' Jilly hesitated, then turned away to gaze out over the moon-silvered rooftops to the sleeping rangelands beyond. 'I suppose it sounds foolish to you, but for some reason I've been thinking of Clint tonight. All night, I've had this strange feeling that he is somewhere close by . . . '

The blacksmith's rugged features softened as he placed a hand on the girl's shoulder. 'No great mystery to me why you might be feeling that way. I realize now you were a whole lot sweeter on that feller than you ever let on, honey.'

She didn't deny it.

'Of course I know what he was and the life he's led, Dad. But from the beginning I felt there was something fine and clean about him, if only he could maybe somehow change his life and allow that side of him to escape. But even if he couldn't do that I think I would still . . . still . . . '

Her voice faded and Ben's tone was sober.

'Look, I understand, honey. I'm not just saying that. But I've got to be honest and say it would never have worked out. I'll be first to admit Clint did a whole heap for us folks and that towards the end I was getting to look on him like he was as fine a man as I ever met. But horse sense kept throwing up all those arguments against him. Like reminding me that his breed never stays any place long, can't be relied upon, just about never makes old bones. Then I could tell Shiloh prized his freedom over most everything else . . . he even told me so once. No, that kind never stays . . . and they sure don't make husbands neither. So, why don't you go to bed and quit daydreaming, huh?'

'I'll go in soon, Dad, I promise.'

'All right,' he said, and kissed the top of her head.

Alone again, Jilly looked up at the moon then let her gaze play over the sleeping landscape. She shook her head. She well knew it was crazy . . . yet was still gripped by that overwhelming feeling that he was near.

She lifted her head and spoke his

name softly, but the murmur of the leaves and the whisper of wind were her only answer.

* * *

The solitary figure standing on the bank of Clearwater Creek five miles from Durant suddenly cocked his head to the night wind. It seemed for a moment he'd heard his name whispered, soft yet clear.

Lonely as smoke on a cold, clear morning, the gunfighter watched the water moving darkly around the stones at his feet as he thought of Marcus Whitman and Cleveland Kain.

On quitting Jawbone and making his way down out of the high country it was with the clear-cut intention of seeking out Marcus Whitman and dragging him off to the low country to face the law, no matter if it killed him.

He still felt this needed to be done — but might the price now be too high since the name Kain had loomed over the high country? As Shakespeare Jones might have said, 'Aye, and there's the rub.'

Kain's appearance was not accidental. Every scrap of common sense argued that. The killer worked for huge money, and the only one with that kind of money up here was Whitman.

He wondered if this had been meant to happen — for the benefit of Clint Shiloh?

His thinking went deep. Would it still be possible for him to make his way into Durant, grab Whitman and haul him off to face the law over his crimes?

He lighted a smoke and dragged deep, grimacing. He knew Whitman had recruited gunmen to replace the ones he'd shot up. They would surely be on the alert, and now their strength would be bolstered by a killer most believed to be invincible.

A dark alternative suggested itself. Forget giving Whitman his hour before a judge. Get in, get one clean shot, then hightail for the lowlands and leave it to

Durant to tidy up behind him?

He shook his head. But even should he succeed and survive, what might be the outcome? The murder — and they would call it that — of a candidate for the State House of Colorado by a notorious man of the gun would have far-reaching effects, perhaps even see the War God Hills placed under martial law as a result.

These were powerful reasons against taking out his gun without thinking it through.

Yet what if he should do nothing? Ride off and leave the town that had been kind to him, and the woman he loved, in the hands of evil men who had proven yet again what they were capable of?

He squared his shoulders and there was a great sorrow in him that had in it the despair of winter as he realized with an air of finality that the one thing he could not do here — was nothing.

He raised his head and felt the world go still. Moonlight hung through the trees and played soft patches of light upon the grass. Two Bits suddenly jerked up his head as though hearing a soft footfall behind him, yet didn't turn his head for fear of what he might see. A long moment of total stillness passed, then the horse relaxed again and swished its tail while the leaves began to stir.

'What was that, old-timer?' Shiloh said in a husky voice. 'Was that the joker with the scythe stepping by?'

The horse grunted and came to him. Shiloh took sugar from his pocket and fed it to him. When he looked up again there was the faintest touch of dawn grey in the eastern sky.

*　*　*

The smoke of the first cigar of the day was trickling from Marcus Whitman's mouth as he quit the store to make his way along to the Greasy Spoon with Kain at his side. It was a sparkling clear morning that gave a man a sharp appetite. Following breakfast at the eatery they would return for the council meeting which by this time was committed to go the way of the dapper man with the derby hat and gloves.

It wasn't until they stepped off the porch into the street that it happened. Suddenly the gunman touched the other's arm and halted.

'What?' Whitman said sharply. He was alert, confident and eager to get on with his day and his plans.

Kain had gone taut, his dark head turning this way and that. He sniffed the air like a hunting dog.

'What is it?' Whitman demanded, sharper now.

'Something not right . . . '

'What?'

Whitman was about to move on when he also felt it. Suddenly there was a sense of something akin to tension in the air, some unidentifiable element which seemed to carry with it a chill despite the sun.

The pair stared around. Four citizens stood across the street by the barber shop, looking across at them. Another bunch of men and women was visible up on the plank-board upper gallery of the Durant Hotel. Everything the two could see appeared normal. Yet surely this was way too quiet for eight-forty-seven on a shiny new morning?

Something was wrong.

Pale and uneasy now, Marcus Whitman felt an odd touch of fear. Yet the moment he glanced at the man beside him it was gone. For what did a man have to fear with Cleveland Kain by his side? Why, that was almost like having the power of life or death at your fingertips.

Even so, he still took a backward step towards the storefront. 'Go take a quick look around, Cleveland, just to be on the sure side. We're not in that much of a hurry.'

The killer's sneer was short-lived. The man who was always cool and arrogant found himself turning his big head this way and that as though he felt he might be missing something.

No. Everything normal.

The gunfighter stepped down and led the way across the street, chin high, arms swinging loosely. Heading for the group before the barber shop he glanced left and right before halting in the centre of the street.

'Jackson! Bell!' he called in his whispery voice, crooking a finger. 'Here!'

The men didn't move. Instantly suspicious, Kain's right hand flew to gunbutt. But he didn't draw. He was more puzzled than angry. These lackeys were trained to jump whenever he said jump. Yet even his imperious summons was having no effect.

'I said come here, you goddamn — '

'It's not them you want to talk to, Kain,' a soft voice said. 'It's me!'

The killer whirled panther-quick and his heavy jaw clicked open.

'Shiloh!'

★   ★   ★

He'd appeared from the alley-mouth with the morning sun at his back

215

throwing his shadow long and thin across the yellow dust before him. He walked neither fast nor slow and folks on the street and those suddenly appearing in windows and doorways along the thoroughfare saw he looked just the same as always, assured, expressionless, moving with silky grace.

When Shiloh paused a moment, a sound like a communal intake of breath whispered along Main. Then he turned to face the store squarely and started forward again.

And while Cleveland Kain stood motionless and seemingly untouched by Shiloh's sudden appearance, the man at Kain's side was visibly coming apart.

This was far too rich for the man who wished to rule. And moving jerkily now a grey-faced Marcus Whitman backed away to the edge of the gallery and stood as though frozen. He'd never expected to see Shiloh again yet here he was — looking maybe even larger than life!

But he wasn't alone, an inner voice

reminded. And one quick glance across at the still motionless Kain saw him instantly begin to recover.

For Kain was surely invincible and looked it as he stood in profile to his challenger, reptilian eyes unblinking in the shadow of his hatbrim. Jaw muscles writhed like little snakes beneath the skin and the fingers of his right hand flexed smoothly, close to his gun.

'You're Shiloh,' he stated, and the other simply nodded.

The tension was shaking Whitman like little electric shocks. 'Take him, Kain! Don't shilly-shally, man! Take him now and talk later — for God's sakes!'

Clint Shiloh halted thirty feet from his adversary. He spoke quietly, yet his words carried. 'Your bloody-handed boss is scared, Kain. But you're not, are you?'

The man with the death's head face shook his head. 'Not of you, Shiloh, nor of any man who ever lived.' A pause, then: 'I know you're good, gunfighter, but that isn't good enough. They said you'd gone. Why did you come back to die?'

Cleveland Kain wasn't trying to bluff or shake his nerve, Clint knew. The man was simply curious. It was as if his death was a foregone conclusion.

'If I die, I won't die alone, Kain.' He sounded sure.

'Your words are coming out of the grave, mister! But I still want my answer before I kill you. You were gone . . . safe. Why did you come back?'

'There's a reason but it's not for you.' Shiloh made a careless gesture. 'But maybe it doesn't have to be this way. You and me . . . we're too fast, too good, to fight one another.'

Kain's jaw lifted fractionally. 'You're saying you want to back down?'

Shiloh shook his head.

'I figured you'd read it that way. No, I'm giving you a chance to back down while you're breathing, maybe end all the killing here and now. But I can see . . . '

He let his voice trail off as he caught the glitter in the other's eye. It told him this man would never quit ... and neither would he. Then he caught a flash of colour from the Flynn house, and his lips shaped her name ...

Next instant, they went for the guns!

Fierce jets of gunflame lanced back and forth through the gunsmoke and onlookers clapped hands to their ears to drown out the sound of lead tearing through blood and bone and living tissue.

The guns clashed for mere moments which seemed an eternity to those on the street. Then came a communal intake of breath washing along Main Street as Cleveland Kain the invincible began to fall.

'He triumphed!' Shakespeare Jones gasped as Clint Shiloh moved forwards through roiling gunsmoke towards the figure in the dust. 'Shiloh, the victorious!'

This was true. With a last exhalation of breath, Kain rolled on to his back and never moved again, face turned to a deep blue sky.

Clint Shiloh stood over him, this momentary image of victor and vanquished frozen indelibly in every watcher's memory. Next moment he toppled and fell, rolling on to his back, the gun slipping from his grasp. The dust received him gently and the voices seemed to come from far away until he felt the hand on his face.

'Clint . . . oh, no, no!'

He couldn't see her, yet he smiled. 'It's all right, Jilly . . . it was worth it . . . '

'Oh why — why did you come back?'

He could see her now. All else was a blur but he saw her face above him.

'Why not?' he quipped, and coughed blood.

'You won't die, Clint Shiloh!' the girl said with sudden fierceness. 'I won't let you, do you hear? I love you, don't you know that?'

He could hear but could not answer. And what he heard told him it had really been worth it. There was no sadness in him, only a kind of singing as a gentle darkness drew him in.

* * *

So this was dying?

Strange, but how could a man think like that if he was dead?

As though suspended in an infinite grey haze, Clint Shiloh seemed to float and dream and once or twice even cursed — until the haze began to lighten and he could see faint shades of colour and felt something very like pain in ribs and leg. Before fingers touched his forehead and he opened his eyes to see — not eternal darkness but rather her face, and at her side Doc Gleeson in a blood-stained white coat ordering him to keep breathing — slow and easy!

And when he found himself thinking, 'Nobody tells Clint Shiloh what to do,' only then did he know he was alive.

* * *

It would not be until later that he would hear how an enraged town had overcome Whitman in the wake of the showdown, then held him three days until the county marshals arrived to escort him back to Denver to face justice.

The day he took his first steps along Main with Jilly Flynn on one side and her father on the other, it seemed most everybody in Durant was there to see and wonder. Some cheered, while one matron confided to her neighbour that she had it on good authority there would be wedding bells soon. And that Jilly, at her patient's insistence, had given his Colt .45 away to an old bum from the hills who would find more use for it than he ever would now.

But it wasn't until Mayor Shakespeare Jones emerged on to the walk of a town reborn that folks felt they'd heard the right words to encompass how they now felt about a man who had come to bring fear but stayed on to save them, when he gestured flamboyantly and boomed: 'Behold you the hero . . .

And the elements so mixed in him,
That nature might stand up and
say to all the world
This was a man!'

Nobody could argue with that. The words of the English dramatist responsible for Jones's nickname had carried across the centuries to a small high country town in America's frontier West to describe Clint Shiloh as they simply knew him to be.

A man.

THE END

Other titles in the
Linford Western Library:

HELL'S COURTYARD

Cobra Sunman

Indian Territory, popularly called Hell's Courtyard, was where bad men fled to escape the law. Buck Rogan, a deputy marshal hunting the killer Jed Calder, found the trail leading into Hell's Courtyard and went after his quarry, finding every man's hand against him. Rogan was also searching for the hideout of Jake Yaris, an outlaw running most of the lawlessness directed at Kansas and Arkansas. Single-minded and capable, Rogan would fight the bad men to the last desperate shot.

SARATOGA

Jim Lawless

Pinkerton operative Temple Bywater arrives in Saratoga, Wyoming facing a mystery: who murdered Senator Andrew Stone? Was it his successor, Nathan Wedge? Or were lawyers Forrest and Millard Jackson, and Marshal Tom Gaines involved? Bywater, along with his sidekick Clarence Sugg, and Texas Jack Logan, faces gunmen whose allegiances are unknown. The showdown comes in Saratoga. Will he come out on top in a bloody gun fight against an adversary who is not only tough, but also completely unforeseen?